THE HEART OF ATLANTA

A Novel

Nick Thomas

Copyright © 2015 Nick Thomas
All rights reserved.

ISBN: 1522977910
ISBN 13: 9781522977919
Library of Congress Control Number: 2016900037
CreateSpace Independent Publishing Platform
North Charleston, South Carolina

This story is dedicated to everyone who shared the Furman campus with me in the early eighties.

CHAPTER ONE

I needed advice. And as I thought about who to consult, I remembered the saying that you choose your advisers according to what you want to hear. There's something to that. I mean at Buchanan there were any number of people I could've gone to with my problem who would surely've preached the straight Southern Baptist line. Get married. Keep the baby. Get a job, and finish school at night. Sacrifice.

But I knew that was all an option. Hell, part of me said the same things. I didn't need that kind of advice. There's no trick to selflessness, no angles to figure. What I didn't know was how to escape from the trap I'd let myself fall into. I needed escape advice.

Once I got straight on what I needed, I knew Marty Lansdowne was my man. Of all the guys in the fraternity, all the people at Buchanan for that matter, Marty was an original, an institution. He'd been in school so long none of the guys could remember him being anything but a senior.

He lived off campus, and in my two years at Buchanan, he only showed up at the fraternity house for special occasions, breezing in more like a successful alum than a perpetual student. But in his day, Marty lived in nearly every room in the house. There were souvenirs of Marty everywhere — fist holes in walls, stolen road signs bolted to ceilings, the big stone fireplace in the corner of the chapter room he and his father built.

Marty was a Greenville local. His family, in fact, lived in the neighborhood right outside the back gate, next to President Brooks' house. Marty's parents and Dr. and Mrs. Brooks were close friends. The four of them barbecued together — the men played golf on the campus links, the ladies drove to Atlanta to shop.

No matter how many Fs, no matter how many incompletes he took, there was no expelling Marty. In the time he'd been in college, he'd paid more tuition than any three normal students. But apart from all that, and apart from the fact that at 24 years old, he'd wrecked more cars than most people own in a lifetime, Marty was a smart, concerned, polite guy. He was the kind of person I wanted to be. You'd never hear him say anything negative about anyone. He treated everyone from the lowest, drunkest freshman to the most senior professor with equal respect. And when he talked to you, he'd find a way to make you feel important, interesting, and by doing that he made you admire him.

The day after I found out for sure Anne was pregnant, I borrowed a buddy's bike and peddled the couple of miles over to Marty's place. He lived in a log and stone cabin set beside a small pond, back in the woods down a long bumpy dirt road. It was the kind of place you'd never know was there unless you'd been shown the way. You couldn't get within a quarter mile of the place without setting off the dog alarm. There were a half-dozen of them, and when they heard you coming they ran at you in a swarm, barking and showing teeth. If you didn't know better, you'd have been smart to turn tail and run. But I did know better. I knew how to deal with them (you stand still with your arms out and your palms up), so I could walk right up to the unlocked house whenever I wanted. That evening though, Marty was out on the porch smoking a cigarette when I rolled up and propped the bike against a tree. I said hey and sat on the top step leading up to the porch. I scratched the dogs behind the ears and patted them on the head and let them sniff me and lick my hands until they got bored and ran down by the pond. Marty finished his smoke and flicked the butt out into the yard.

"What's the problem, Jimmy?" he said after a while. He could see I was upset.

"I screwed up," I said. "Anne McGowen's pregnant."

"You sure?"

That question caught me off guard. Suddenly, I caught the slightest whiff of hope, the hint of a possible out. That was Marty for you, and that was the kind of thing I was after. God, I wanted out. But was I sure? Yeah. I was pretty sure. She cried when she told me. And I don't know why she'd lie. I don't know if she took one of those drug-store tests. And I doubt she went to the doctor. But she was late. Way late.

"Yeah," I said. "I'm pretty sure."

"OK. OK." He walked down and sat beside me. "Do you know how far along she is?"

"Two months. Something like that."

"OK. Good. It's best to know as soon as possible."

I felt terrible. But in a way it was getting better, like Marty was helping me carry the weight. Keep going, I thought. Tell me what I should do.

"How's Anne reacting?" he asked.

"Well, I think she's pretty scared. She's been crying a lot, and missing some classes."

Marty sat and thought for a while. He looked at the trees and the dogs and the old, dull red Pontiac GTO he had up on blocks in the side yard. I sat quietly and just waited, not wanting to disturb him. It was like I had programmed a computer and was waiting for the answer to emerge on a strand of ticker tape. He almost said something, but then he hesitated, switched gears.

"Do you love her?" he said.

"I think I do," I said after some thinking. "I tell her I do, and she tells me back. But that doesn't mean I wanna jump off a bridge or anything. I mean, I love being with her, and I love doing for her. I think I'd even like to marry her some day. But not now. Not right now."

"You think she'd get an abortion if you asked her?"

"I don't know. And I'm not sure I have any right to ask her."

"You're right. You can't tell her to, you can't order her to. It's her decision. But you can tell her how you feel."

"I don't know how to feel." I didn't want to be responsible for killing a baby. Jesus. But I didn't want to be a father either. For a minute I thought I was gonna panic. Run. Bawl. It was a rushing, falling feeling. This was the first time the choice seemed so clear. I guess I'd been hoping for a way out, but there wasn't any. Only two bad choices. Neither one would get me anywhere worth going. But then I knew, without reasoning, without thinking it through, that I didn't want a baby. I was nineteen years old, for Christ's sake. And I didn't mean to get her pregnant. I tried . . .

I took one of Marty's cigarettes from the pack on the porch rail and touched a match to it. "Marty. Tell me what to do. What should I do?"

"Well, the first thing," he said, "the main thing, is that it's not up to us."

"Us," I thought. What did he mean, "us?" Did he mean guys in general, or him and me specifically? It wasn't clear, but somehow I knew, from the tone of his voice I guess, that he meant the second thing. Marty was letting me in on something about himself.

Then it hit me, the reason I'd come to Marty. Somehow I knew, without really knowing, that Marty had been through the same mess. I wanted to hear his story. I wanted to know if there was any going on after something like this. But I didn't think it was right to ask.

"Two hundred bucks," Marty said finally. "That's what it costs at the clinic downtown. And I think if you want any chance at holding on to her, you ought to pay. If you don't have it, I can loan it to you."

"No," I said. "I got it. It's still early enough in the term."

As I peddled home in the starlight along the bumpy dirt road, I decided Marty was right. An abortion was the way to go. Nobody's interest was going to be served by having this baby — not mine, not Anne's, not our parents'. I thought about God. In a way, I felt as though I had decided to give up — give up my chance at living the kind of life that would pay off in the end, give up the long, running dialogue I'd kept with Him since I was old enough to sit still and fold my hands and pray. I'd always tried to run my life the way they taught me. I'd been saying goodnight to Him every night, just before falling asleep, for as long as I could remember. Even when I realized I was going to sleep with Anne, I figured He would understand I loved her and didn't mean any offense by what I did.

But this was different. This was pure self-interest, pure self-preservation. I knew this wasn't what He wanted me to do, but I didn't care. Well, I cared, but I was gonna do it anyway. I was gonna push for the abortion, even though I knew it was unforgivable. I was pissed I even had to think about Him. He knows me. He knows my heart. And if He didn't like my decision, I thought, then we'd both just have to live with that.

CHAPTER TWO

Less than a year and a half before all my bad luck started, I'd arrived at Buchanan expecting the best. My parents and I packed my gear into my mom's old Country Squire station wagon, and we made the twelve-hour drive from Wrights Beach, Florida to Greenville, South Carolina and Buchanan University. We arrived after sundown, the night before I was to check into my dorm, so we took a room in the Downtown Hyatt. The lobby was an expanse of polished wood and palm trees and other tropical plants open to the moonlight beneath a four-story-high glass ceiling. Near the cocktail-lounge corner of the lobby, a man in a tuxedo played a grand piano that sat on a circular, concrete island in the middle of a pool-water-blue fountain.

In the morning, we dressed, ate some pancakes in the hotel restaurant, and then knocked around the shops downtown. I took note of all the bars and pool halls. My mom spotted a church, and we went in and prayed for a minute. On the way out, Mom spoke to a lady dusting the pews and found out the name of a priest I could call if I wanted to join up.

In the afternoon, we drove out to Buchanan to move my gear into the dorm. We arrived early, so we detoured up Paris Mountain, the wooded peak that stands guard over the campus. I still couldn't get over the Carolina landscape — the rolling hills filled with dogwoods and oaks and pines, the deep green kudzu vines that blanket acres at a stretch along the highway, the clear cool sky that hangs close overhead and then stretches off behind the Appalachian foothills on the horizon. It made me smile. It confirmed my idea that flat, scrubby Florida wasn't the whole world, that there was a lot more to see, a lot more to do.

When we reached the top of Paris Mountain, we parked and walked out onto a broad outcropping of rock, surveying the scene. The campus was spread below us, and Greenville, with its few tall buildings, hovered on the horizon to the left. A cool wind tousled our hair. Mom took a scarf from her purse and tied it into a hood over her head to keep everything in place. She squinted in the bright light and seemed frail to me with the whole globe spread out below her. I loved her then and worried about what she'd do without me. My Dad had picked up a handful of rocks and was firing them out into the sky and watching them drop out of sight into the pines. He tossed me one, and I let it fly out in the direction of the golf course, on the far right side of the campus.

I stopped and looked down at the campus' central lake with the bell tower rising from the tip of a narrow peninsula, the boys' dorms above the lake and the girls' dorms below, the common buildings off to the left — the library, the student union, the dining hall, the auditorium, and the long row of classroom buildings — and to the far left, the gym and football stadium.

After some time, we got back into the wagon and wound our way back down the mountain and out onto the interstate. When we saw the sign for the Buchanan exit, we branched off the highway onto a curving, one-way lane that circled back under the highway and through a thick patch of trees. The street was painted with a series of big purple horseshoes, a symbol of the school's football team, the Horsemen. Then the trees opened up and we were at the main entrance, a solid wrought iron gate connected to a red brick guardhouse. A brass plaque on the structure read: BUCHANAN UNIVERSITY, CRISTO ET DOCTRIAE (For God and Learning), EST. 1826.

My eyes bugged when out of the guardhouse stepped a pretty blonde girl in a short purple cheerleader's uniform. Dad turned and looked at me. I gave him the eyebrows.

We inched up closer and mom rolled her window down. The cheerleader hunched down and looked through my mom's window at me. She asked for my name. Mom and I spoke at the same time. "James Macy." The cheerleader smiled, consulted her clipboard, and put a check by my name. She welcomed us and pointed the way to the boy's dorms.

Dad circled the Squire around a big fountain bordered with flowerbeds, and we rolled slowly down a tree-lined lane, past the deserted classroom buildings, past the silent library with its three-story-high Georgian columns, and down to the Gymnasium. Then we took a right and climbed a hill, passing the wide, smooth playing fields, and up to the boys' dorms. That was where the activity was.

Cars and trucks were parked everywhere — on the sidewalks, on the grass, anywhere there was room — hazard lights flashing and trunk hoods raised. People were moving in every direction, hauling trunks and suitcases, stereos and golf bags and mini refrigerators into the maze of red brick buildings. My heart pumped hard. I couldn't believe I was gonna jump into the middle of this on my own, and that before the sun went down, my folks will have kissed me on the forehead and be on the interstate heading for home.

As we circled the complex trying to figure out where I belonged, I checked out the other guys. They all seemed pleased enough.

They walked around in gangs of six or eight. In a field beyond the dorms, sloping down to the bank of the lake, a cluster of guys were throwing a Frisbee, running and jumping and rolling in the grass. I got the feeling my mom was getting nervous. After all, this was it. This was the end of my childhood. This was college, the thing we had been talking about ever since I was old enough to understand the word. The preliminaries were over, the Catholic school and middle school and high school, the music lessons, the soccer and baseball, the garbage can carrying and grass raking, the time limits and permission getting. To her, I guess it seemed like I'd be the same knucklehead who couldn't think far enough ahead to keep gas in his car. Only now I wouldn't have anyone to watch over me. But to me it seemed like an escape — not from my parents, but from being a kid. I knew I didn't know everything. But I also knew I'd learned everything I could in Wright's Beach, and that if I'd stayed where I was, I'd have been doomed to a life of repetition. Yes, I was out and that felt good.

CHAPTER THREE

Two hours later, I was moved into my room on the freshman hall, and my parents were gone. I'd set up my stereo, and I sat there listening to a Pablo Cruise tape, watching that same bunch of guys playing Frisbee on the west lawn when I heard a knock at the door. I opened up and my new roommate Jay was standing there grinning with his arms full of shirts on hangers. He was half a foot shorter than me and a little stocky, with short sandy hair and narrow, vacant eyes that gave the impression that he was thinking something complicated. He had a girl with him. Her name was Anne — my Anne — and she stood there holding a stereo speaker.

We said our hellos, and I took the speaker from her. I thought she was beautiful. She wore Levis and a T-shirt and a string of gold beads. Her hair was dark and thick and hung below her shoulders. Her face was smooth and friendly. Naturally, though, I assumed that she and Jay were a couple. So I just acted regular friendly toward her and didn't think much more about it. It wasn't until after we got all Jay's things moved in and then helped Anne move in to the girls' dorm across the lake that I got Jay alone and found out that she and Jay were not boyfriend and girlfriend, but just friends from high school, and that Anne was dating a fellow who was in his second year of law school at the University of Georgia.

I saw a lot of Jay and Anne those first few weeks. The two of them stuck together, and since none of us knew many people at that early date, the three of us made a convenient little gang. We'd go eat pizza or go to a movie or go drink beer at this bar near campus called the Stump, where you could go out back on nice days and throw horseshoes.

By the time we got settled into class and did meet a few people, fall rush started, and Jay and I jumped in. I'm not sure why it meant so much to me, but from the first day, from before the first day of college, I knew I wanted to be part of a fraternity, I wanted to be part of something big, something important, something that just by my being a part of it would let people know I was a person worth knowing, a friend worth having.

When it started, I liked it as much as I thought I would. I liked the feeling of being courted by these groups of older guys, feeling as if they thought I was a prime target, the cream of the freshman class. And once the rhythm of rush began, each night, each party, was a swirl of loud music and beer and grain punch and shouted conversations with people from all over the country, people who looked like me, dressed like me, shared my way of looking at the world. I felt the thrill of seeing myself reflected back and liking what I saw. In those few weeks of parties, I checked myself over completely. I talked about everything I had ever seen or read or thought about and carefully measured the response I got back. Was I smart? Yes. Was I likable? Yes. Compassionate? Yes. Too Religious? No. Moral enough? Yes. Was I on my way to something good, some ultimate reward — a good job, a beautiful wife, a big house and a happy family? Yes, definitely yes.

The strangest thing about fraternity rush was the way guys sorted themselves out. I'd always figured the fraternities did the picking, but what I saw was different, and it taught me something about people — they excluded themselves from things, they blackballed themselves.

There was a good guy from my hall, Stuart Avery, and at the beginning of things, he went to all the parties with Jay and me. The three of us were practically interchangeable, one from Florida, one from Georgia, and one from Tennessee, slightly different accents, but besides that we were the same — we wore the same kinds of cloths, listened to the same music, and admired the same girls. But somehow, as rush wore on and it became clear which fraternities were the top-notchers (had the biggest parties and the prettiest little sisters, won the most intermurals), as Jay and I made our move to go for the top, Stuart split off.

When the time came to go around from room to room meeting the brother of the two top frats — the ATOs and the SAEs — Stuart begged off, citing homework. And at the parties, Stuart gravitated to the back rooms, shooting pool or throwing darts, instead of making himself known. It was like he was trying to fail, even though I knew he wanted a bid from the ATOs, even though I knew he wanted to be liked.

How could a guy like Stuart come to college, a place where he knew no one, a place where he had no history, a place where he could be anyone or anything he wanted, and put himself in the back seat? It was like he was holding up a sign saying: Hey, I'm Stuart, nothing special, nothing much to look at, nothing much interesting to say. He took himself out of the running.

So a month later, Stuart and I are wearing different color pledge pins. He's part of an open-door Christian frat, and Jay and I are ATOs. And between classes and parties and pledge duties, Stuart and I get where we hardly ever see each other, and when we do there's nothing much to say. My inclination is to feel sorry for him. But I can't do that. He'd made up his own mind. And I couldn't change everything I was doing just so I could keep hanging out with him.

What do you do with someone like that? I remember my dad telling me about his decision to stay in Wright's Beach and sell insurance while his brother, my Uncle Ted, moved to Tampa to work for a bank. It was the fishpond theory. There were more opportunities in the city, more money, and the chance to move up and up and up. But you're never the big fish, the lunker. No matter how high you go, you're never on top. In a small town, you're it, you're the top of the food chain.

Maybe that was close to the way Stuart was thinking. Maybe he thought he'd get lost in the crowd if he went with Jay and me. Maybe that was true. But what was an 18-year-old guy doing without ambition?

CHAPTER FOUR

Apart from the time I spent that first fall on rush and the time I spent hanging with Jay and Anne and the time I spent studying and attending class, there was one other activity that commanded my attention. That activity's name was Ginny.

I met Ginny during the first week of classes. She worked in the cafeteria frying eggs. I was standing back in the line with my tray and my silverware and napkin. She raised her eyes from the grill and shot me a quick little smile, and then went back to work cracking eggs into puddles of buttery grease. She had blonde hair and pale skin, and her face was beaded with a fine sweat, like she had just finished a set of tennis. When I reached the front of the line, she kept her head down for a second and then looked up at me and said, "Hi, Jimmy," as she slid a couple of sunny side ups onto my plate. I smiled, I guess, and then walked away.

Until that fall, I had spent my entire life in Florida, and the chilly Carolina air felt like winter to me. A few leaves were already starting to turn orange and fall. All the other new kids were out walking in a hundred directions, dressed in bright new sweaters and faded high school jeans and lugging bright vinyl backpacks stuffed with unread books. They all smiled. Everyone smiled in the nicest way. The campus was clean, and the grass was cut, and the fallen leaves were raked into neat little piles. As I walked to humanities, I tried to figure out how that pretty blonde egg girl knew my name. Jay was already sitting in class when I arrived, so I went up and parked next to him. I took out my books, and when class started, I listened hard and tried to write down everything my professor said.

When class was over, the egg girl was sitting in the hall waiting for me. I walked up to her, and she said hello and explained that she had seen my picture in the freshman face book, and that she was from Florida too, and didn't I miss it already? I told her no and meant it. I was happy to be away, I said. I was ready for something good to happen to me, and I was more than willing for her to help me if she could.

Soon enough, I discovered that she had been waiting for something good too. And as it turned out, she thought I was that good thing. Over roast beef and green bean dinners at the dining hall, and beer and cigarette evenings at the Stump, she explained how she had never had any fun, and how really, to be really honest, she felt as though she had just been born. She was always saying "really, to be really honest," and when she did she would knit her brow in a way that made me believe what she said.

I believed her dad was a prominent doctor who screwed around a lot, including one Tampa Bay Buccaneer cheerleader. I believed her mother had breast cancer. I believed her house was big and expensive with marble floors and thick wood paneling, and that all the shutters were kept closed and all the blinds drawn, and that for the past three years her mom hadn't left the house except to go to her doctor, and that she had not worn a dress in as long, and that she spent hours at a time sitting at a Steinway in their living room playing the songs from Barbara Streisand's movie: *A Star is*

Born. I believed Ginny when she said she loved me too, and when she kissed me, I ran all the way back to the dorm. I felt way ahead of the game. I had only been at Buchanan a week and a pretty girl already loved me. Jay's suitcases were barely unpacked.

As fall pressed on, I found that having Ginny around was a convenience. There were certain events where it looked good for a guy to have a date, and all I had to do was call her, and she'd be there. There was no question of her turning me down, no possibility that she'd have plans or another date. For some reason, she was devoted to me. I gotta admit there were some things I liked about her. I appreciated the fact she was slim and blonde and pretty, and that the Florida influence on the way she dressed (there was always some extra bit of skin showing) made her seem somehow exotic next to the boyish Carolina girls. I also liked the fact that no one else seemed to know her (as far as I knew, I was her only companion), and if by occasionally bringing her around I gave the impression that my social circles extended beyond the Greek system, that there was more to me than it at first appeared, it was not for me to deny. And if the price I had to pay for having her at my disposal was having her believe there was more between us than there really was, if she wanted to consider me her steady, that was OK with me — not great, but OK. It was not my plan to mislead her. It was more that I just had other things on my mind. If she wanted to use me, my name, for her own purposes, that was alright — no one else was using it. Not yet.

CHAPTER FIVE

By the time Christmas came and went, Jay and I had gone from unknowns to fixtures on campus. No two guys were more widely known or widely liked. No two guys smiled wider or drank harder, staid up later or crashed on more strange couches. No two guys listened harder or remembered names better or were more willing to help out, no matter the reason, no matter the cause. In a way we were celebrities. For a while it took over everything. From our new room on the attic level of the fraternity house across to lake, each day began and ended with hand shaking and yelled greetings across lawns, earnest conversations and meaningless chatter. It was like we were running for political office. It felt sweet.

I was building myself into a model citizen. Each day I traded in some doubt for a new confidence, some ignorance for a newer, more complete understanding. In a way I felt like an actor studying for a role. When I heard someone say something interesting, or act in a way I found appealing, I'd grab onto it, isolate it, analyze it, and then work it into my repertoire. The thing I remember the most about that time was how fascinated I was with everything. I was flattered when a professor would talk to me in the hall about some book or idea or when a downtown bum marked me as a likely source to throw a couple of coins. Everything I heard, everything I saw was filled with layer after layer of meaning, of interest, and everything I learned doubled back on itself and buttressed everything else. There were times, I swear, when, as I walked across campus smiling and waiving, I could stop it all, freeze the world in place and look at it from above, examine it. It was mine.

The more my celebrity grew, the less I felt like dealing with Ginny. Really, from the start, I knew she wasn't for me. There was something about the quick way she latched on to me, the way I instantly became the center of her life, the way she wrapped her thin frame around me and kissed me dramatically when we danced in front of the guys at a frat party, the way she'd parade around campus grinning and holding my arm. I didn't trust her. I always felt she wanted something from me I couldn't give. It's not that I was anything so special. I didn't play football or basketball. I wasn't rich.

There were times I would sit and talk to Ginny, times when she was tired or frustrated, and I could tell she would turn off her brain and let the angry words and thoughts of her mother take over. It was like she took comfort in the familiar maze of pain where smiles were a cover for lies and love was water that could be given or withheld or cruelly trickled to the thirsty. Somehow, when Ginny became her mother, I could see how her dad must feel. What was it about the vulnerable that made them so easy to hurt? What was it that made it so much sadder to see a golden Labrador dead on the roadside than a ribby mutt? When Ginny was at her worst, it was like she didn't have the first drop of goodness inside her. It was like she would want to siphon all the spirit out of you if you let her, just like you'd figure a sorry dog would eat anything it could get its teeth on, while a happy family dog knew not to mess with the cat's food or the steaks on the picnic table by the grill. And knowing that Ginny was so dependent on me for happiness, so blind, brought out feelings in me that I could hardly recognize, feelings I never felt when I was with Anne. It could be something as simple as asking, no, making Ginny walk back to the girls' dorm alone. When Anne visited, it went without saying that we would straighten up our room, buy her a soda, and then walk her back home later. But with Ginny, I'd just hear an unannounced knock on the door. I'd let her in and continue doing what I was doing.

When Anne visited, she would leave the room feeling fuller. When Ginny visited, she would somehow take something away.

It was later that spring, almost time for Beach Bash, the fraternity's annual weekend in Myrtle Beach, when I found out that Anne and her lawyer had split up. Jay told me they had been planning to be together in Atlanta in the summer, but that the lawyer had taken a job offer in New York. Anne was pretty upset about it, and one night, after I had been at a KA party, Anne cornered me. She had been at the party too, and had been drinking. When she came up to me, I thought for a second she was going to try something. Instead, she started crying and telling me how upset she was about breaking up with the lawyer, how they had been together since she was in tenth grade. She told me how she had to buck her parents to get them to allow her to see a guy that was so much older. She told me that she had been thinking she was going to marry this guy for so long that she felt like she had been married and that she was going through a divorce. Then she held on to me and cried. I put my arms around her and let it all happen.

I never told Ginny right out that things were over between us. I was afraid it'd hurt her — I mean not just hurt her feelings or upset her — but really hurt her, injure her. Ginny had that lunatic edge to her personality that made you believe she was capable of many things, many questionable things. And if I had cared a little bit more about her, or a little bit less about myself, I can see where I might have felt obligated to stay with her. It's not that I thought she'd kill herself, it was more that I thought she might suffer a deep kind of disappointment that would crush the little bit of faith she had. Ginny explained to me once how she didn't look forward to anything, how she never understood it when people talked about change being for the better. She said if you dread change, and something bad happens, at least you can be happy it passed. She told me she was happy when she was with me and she didn't want anything to happen, but that she figured it probably would.

I didn't want to add to her cynicism, but I also wanted to be rid of her. I cared about her, her soul, but I just couldn't be there every day to tend it. Somehow it seemed less cruel to excuse myself one Friday night at a time. There was always a reason, and if I wrapped it around the fraternity, she understood. Ginny was comfortable in the back seat.

And just as there was no abrupt end to things with Ginny, there was no bright-line start to things with Anne. In the weeks after her break-up with her lawyer, we just kept getting together to do little things on Thursday or Friday nights, the way we'd been doing all year. The difference was that Jay had just started dating this girl named Kelly Rocker from Charleston, and he was staying busy with her much of the time. So what had been Jay and Anne and me, an established gang of friends, became, on nights when Jay couldn't make it, dates — friendly, happy dates that started with smiles and ended with comfortable, pressureless kisses. We'd been hugging friends for so long that we became girlfriend and boyfriend without negotiation. She just decided, and it happened.

In the weeks leading up to the fraternity's annual weekend in Myrtle Beach, I knew Anne was going to be my date, but I wasn't sure just what kind of date. Would she room with the girls, or would we stay together? And if we did share a room, would we keep things the way they had been, or would we push past that?

Was it time to grow up — and act that way? Would she tell me she loved me? And if she did, would it mean she loved me then or that she loved me for good? I knew I loved her once and for good, but that didn't mean I felt ready to sleep with her. I guess that's because I loved her in a way that I didn't want to take a chance and upset her by pushing things along too quickly. Or maybe it was because I never got past seeing things the way they put them to me when I was a boy.

CHAPTER SIX

The fact that she slept with me, the fact that she told me she loved me and I told her back was all that mattered of our freshman trip to Myrtle Beach. Everything else was background music. And when it was over and we were back at Buchanan, with final exams looming, and a long summer beyond it, things became more serious. My grades were down, and my classes, which had become quiet places to rest, started sneaking into my dreams. My textbooks still smelled of binders glue, and they still folded back closed on their own when I took my hands off them.

When I put my head down and tried to study, nothing happened. I read chapter after chapter, late into the night, wired on cheekfulls of Red Man. But when I woke in the morning, Anne was the only thing clear in my head. The things I'd read the night before were like memories of half-heard conversations — I remembered sort of what they were about, but the details, the specifics, what few I could remember, floated around unattached to any larger understanding.

Two weeks later exams were over and I found myself back in Florida hanging off a ladder, sweating in the sun, painting under the eves of my parents' house. I spent my off time at the beach, drinking beer and laughing when I could, and then hurrying home, making sure I was there by 11:00 so I could call Anne when the rates went down. That was the only time of the day when I didn't hurt wanting to be with her. Instead, when we talked, I felt sad but comfortable, and lonely. My eyes teared up and the swallowing part of my throat felt raw.

My dad was paying me five bucks an hour for the work I did around the house, and apart from the little I spent on gas and beer, I saved everything I made to buy a plane tickets to go to Atlanta.

It was late in June by the time I'd save enough for a trip. My mom wasn't too happy about my going, so I didn't ask her for a ride to the airport. Instead, I got an old friend to give me a lift up to Orlando. I spent a nervous hour in the air and then we set down in the middle of a summer storm. Getting off the plane, I felt a warm mist on my face where the wind blew the rain through the seam where the cabin door met the mouth of the tunnel that led to the terminal. As I walked — slowly behind other passengers carrying luggage — I felt more and more jumpy. Then finally I came to the end of the tunnel and saw the people waiting, and I scanned their faces, and then there she was, behind some folks, off to the side, smiling sweet. There she was. Seeing her did something to me, something strong. I walked up and hugged her, felt her body against mine. I didn't dare kiss her. It'd been a while, and I wasn't sure it'd be natural, comfortable. So I waited. She slipped her hand into mine, and I could feel it all, the thin delicate bone, the warm soft flesh.

Jay was waiting for us down by the baggage carousel with a short, friendly-looking girl who I later found out was named Sue Myers, a high school friend of Anne and Jay. Jay was happy to see me, and he grinned and shook my hand hard and patted me on the shoulder and introduced me to Sue as his best friend. By the time the buzzer sounded and the parade of luggage began, the four of us were talking and laughing, me with my arm around Anne's shoulder. With the weekend spread before me and with Anne and Jay beside me, I felt a tingling, whole-body satisfaction that changed me, converted me. I knew there was nothing that special about either of them, but they were mine, my center. I loved them.

Back at home, I felt worse that before, estranged, exiled. My mom started giving me a hard time. She rode me for spending every dollar I earned. She rode me for not being home nights, for missing dinners. I think the thing that bothered her most was that she could tell I was miserable being in my own home, and that all I lived for was to scrape together enough money to go back and see Anne.

Somewhere around the Fourth, she started in on me about the phone bills I was running up. She told me I had to pay them out of my Atlanta money. We battled and I cussed her, but she didn't bend and I ended up paying. Later that week, my dad took me aside and told me he knew I was hurting and that he'd go two dollars to my one on my plane tickets. I thanked him and shook his hand. I knew my mom had okayed the subsidy, but the fact that she couldn't support me to my face hurt.

By the last part of August, most of my beach friends had gone back to their state schools — University of Florida, Florida State. I wasn't due back until September 9. I still hadn't saved a cent, and that ate at my mom. But my dad stepped in again and made me another deal. There was a long line of Brazilian pepper trees growing along one side of our property, and dad said he'd pay me a thousand bucks if I could get them cut down and burned by the time I left. I said okay, and the next day, a Saturday, he and I drove down to Ft. Pierce to the equipment store and picked out an extra rugged chain saw, five extra blades, a sharpening file, and three cases of oil. On the way back home, we talked and he tried to explain the reason my mom was having so much trouble letting go of me.

The next morning I dragged out of bed early and started the long job, cracking the morning quiet with the shrill whine of the chain saw. By the time I quit for lunch, I had over fifteen feet cleared and the cuttings piled in the middle of the pasture. I was covered with dirt, and my arms and legs and sunburnt neck were punctuated with bug bite. But somehow I was enjoying myself. Mom seemed happy to see me working so hard, and I was happy knowing my reunion with Anne was not too far away, and that when I got back to school I'd have some money to take her out and show her a good time. There was also something about the labor, something about the starting at one end of a row of trees and seeing them fall one at a time, the clear progress of it that made me smile. It wasn't easy to see any other progress in my life. My time passed slowly, and I spent most of it brooding over the things I didn't have, the things I wasn't doing, the places I couldn't be. But this was different. These smelly sappy trees were something tangible, something besides time between me and where I wanted to be. And they were something I could attack, something I could spent my frustration on.

On the Thursday before the Saturday I was set to drive back north, I yanked the saw to life for one last time and dropped the last tangled tree. I dragged each branch to the middle of the pasture and leaned each one against the pile that I had been stacking for almost two weeks. Then I took a gallon of kerosene and circled the pile, dousing the driest branches and then pouring a path of fuel out away from pile. Then I touched a match to the end of the trail and watched the flame walk toward the pile. The whole stack seemed to catch at once. The fuel burned wildly, the flames bending with the afternoon breeze, sending the leaves on the newly cut trees snapping and popping into the air. But that was over in less than a minute, and the dark smoke from the kerosene nearly stopped, and the only real way you could tell anything was happening was to watch the ripples of the rising heat and the wavy way it made the trees in the distance appear. Then the smoke started again, whiter and faster rising than before. Then you could see flames at the core of the pile, and then the flames reached out and grabbed more and more of the wood until finally the whole great pile was one flame, one fire, pulling and puffing and leaping high into the air. Then the summer was finally, finally over.

CHAPTER SEVEN

In Catholic school, they taught me that one of God's gift to us was the inability to remember pain. I've always believed that. I know it's true of physical, toothache, scraped-knee pain — you can remember it was there, but the sensation, the feeling doesn't come back — and I think it's mostly true of emotional pain. I don't know whether the bad feelings flow out of you or whether they crawl into some chamber in the back of your brain, behind a lock you don't hold the key to. I guess it doesn't matter, except for my question of whether what's true for pain is also true for pleasure. And if the inability to remember pleasure is the price we pay to keep from hurting, I'm not sure how good the gift is after all.

All this is really just to say that the time I was happiest — that second fall when Anne and Jay and I were together and everything was right, when the wanting was over and the having was on me — is the time I can remember the least about. I could tell you about some of the things that happened — the football games, the parties, the nights sitting in the dark with Anne on the cool grassy hill that sloped down to the intramural fields — but that doesn't bring it back for me, so I'm not sure anything I could say could let you know. All I know is that the feeling is still there, swimming somewhere in my head. And sometimes I'll see or hear something, and it will chip off a piece of that good feeling, and for 2 or 3 seconds that little bit will wash over me like a sweet breeze. The trouble is that I don't know what those things, those triggers, are. I can tell you that sometimes when I'm walking down the street I'll see a car — it's usually small, a sports car, in a faded and scratched dark brown — that will remind me of a toy car I had when I was very young. I can't remember the specific little Hot Wheels toy, but the feeling is unmistakable; it's sweet and big and comfortable and in a little-kid way, ambitious and glamorous and full of possibilities.

Maybe the lesson is that you have to forget a thing completely before the essence, the boiled down sweetness can come back to you. It's possible that when you still think you remember, you try so hard to impose some structure on the memory that you end up drowning out the feeling. If there's any truth to this, then I think it's an encouraging thought about growing old. I can think of worse things than letting the complicated details of your life slip away and letting the sweet, unattached feelings sweep over you. But I'm not an old man yet, and though the things I'm telling you about happened a good while ago, I can still remember a lot of the details, and worse, I can't help trying to analyze them. And I guess that's the quickest way to kill the feeling of something. So I end up loosing on both ends — I can't put the memories to bed and just enjoy the leftover feelings when they come, and I can't make any sense of the things I can't forget. I can't learn anything I can hold on to. All I can do is go over and over it and try to find out where I made the wrong turn.

All I know is that by the early part of November the leaves were turning and falling again and the nights were cold and the good part was over. Anne was pregnant for sure, and before long I'd had my discussion with Marty and decided that an abortion was the best way to go. After that, everything started to fall apart, and I started all this looking back.

CHAPTER EIGHT

The Buchanan student union is a modern brick and glass building that stands on the lakeshore between the men's dorms and the dining hall. And every evening around six, text books are dog-eared and set aside, stereos are silenced, basketballs are tossed on bunks, and a slow parade of unenthusiastic diners begins at the dorms and trails its way down the hill and through and out the union, through a formal rose garden and into the dining hall.

It was early November, sophomore year, and the first serious snatch of cold had come. I was walking to dinner with a few of my fraternity brothers. The leaves on the dogwoods were shades of red and orange and yellow, and on the sidewalks the fallen leaves shattered under our feet as if made of thin glass. As I opened the door to the union, the heat wrapped around me and pulled me inside.

When I checked my mailbox, there was an envelope from my mom. Inside there was a little note about nothing and a dividend check from Merrill Lynch for two hundred and eleven dollars. It was strange. In my pocket I had a check already made out for two hundred dollars, the money I needed for Anne. So I split off from the guys and went into the bank, and instead of cashing the check in my pocket, I cashed the Merrill Lynch check and skimmed off the eleven-dollar profit.

I stopped by the fireplace on my way out and thought for a while. I don't remember thinking about whether what I was doing was right or wrong. The decision was already made. I was mostly just worried about Anne, worried that it would hurt, worried because I wouldn't be with her to promise her things, to prop her up.

After a while, I walked back outside on my way to meet Anne at the dining hall. The sun had dipped below the tree line across the lake and the wind had kicked up. The temperature was dropping noticeably, and everybody heading to dinner hustled, their hands in their pockets, their chins tucked down into their sweaters.

I was passing through the rose garden when I heard Anne's voice creep into my ears. I turned and saw her sitting on the brick stairs that lead up toward the library. I hurried over. I didn't say anything. I just walked over and sat down beside her and put my arms around her. She slipped her hands into the pocket of my down vest.

"I've been waiting for you," she said. "I've been thinking . . . well, wondering . . . ."

"Listen, don't worry," I cut her off, I guess. "Here. Take this." I took the envelope with the money out of my pocket and handed it to her. "This'll take care of things."

She took the envelope without looking at it.

"I know it'll be tough," I said. "But I love you, and I know you're doing right."

She looked at me and stiffened her chin and nodded a little yes.

We walked the rest of the way to the dining hall. She walked with her arms around me and her head on my chest. Inside, the big room was warm and steamy, full of the clatter of silverware on plates and the static of hundreds of conversations. Anne and I gathered our trays and forks and knives, and took our place in the line. As the line moved, we turned the corner and I saw Ginny standing over a steaming vat, dishing out mashed potatoes.

She looked over and saw me with Anne, and then looked back down at her potatoes. As we passed, out of spite or pride or something, I held up two fingers, just to let her know how things stood. Ginny handed over the potatoes without ever looking at Anne.

With our trays full, Anne and I walked back out into the big hall, past the long fraternity table where we usually sat and laughed and chucked peas at people, and over to the wall where there were small tables and you could be alone and talk.

We found a two-seater by the window. The lake across the lawn was barely visible in the fading light. The floodlights from the roof of the dining hall cut big semi-circles on the lawn. We sat quietly for a while, and then talked in low voices about the papers we had due in our American History class. Anne talked a little about her report. She was writing about a civil rights case from the 60s called the Heart of Atlanta case, where the Supreme Court decided that hotel owners had to rent rooms to black folks. Anne said she thought it was the right thing to do, but she didn't believe any of the nicer places in the city paid much attention to it. Besides, she said, the best hotels are so expensive, only rich people can stay there — and that's a kind of segregation you can't legislate away.

After I finished my fried chicken and mashed potatoes and green beans, I sat back and sipped on a cup of hot tea and watched Anne talk. We were both 19 years old, but she seemed older. It wasn't that she looked older — her face was smooth and even and full of color. It wasn't that she particularly acted older. There was just something good in her eyes, something long-range, something that pulled me toward wanting to be an adult. Right then I would rather have held her all night in a cozy bed than have had tickets to the best concert. Then I thought again about how she was going to have to go in for the operation — alone, scared. I thought how the pain would sit in her soft little stomach, and how she would be sad, and burdened with the thought that our little baby could have grown up and done something that needed doing. I thought about how she'd have something in common — the abortion — with girls that were nothing like her — not as smart or as pretty or as well brought up.

Suddenly, the noise in the big room stopped. I looked into the center of the room and saw everyone was looking at the windows. I turned, and in the light outside I saw sparse flakes of falling snow. It was as if the whole room — eleven or twelve hundred kids — was willing the snow to fall, willing something to happen. It was as if the snow would mark the end of something bad or the start of something good. I didn't know which. But I felt what I imagined they were all feeling, and I wanted the snow to fall.

And the snow did fall — first in more and more ashy flakes blowing from side to side and even upward, and then, finally, in heavy, doughy flakes. Something was happening. The noise and the clatter in the room rose back up and a long line formed at the conveyor belt where you put your tray and your dirty dishes. Gangs of people gathered to go play in the new snow. I saw the guys from the fraternity milling around, thinking, I guess, what to do to best take advantage of the situation. I wanted to go get in on the action. I wanted to run and slip and slide down hills. I looked at Anne to see how she was reacting. She was sitting calmly, staring out at the blanket of white that was forming on the ground.

"You about through?" I said.

"Umm?" she said still looking out the window.

"You ready?" The gang was heading out the door. I was keyed up and kinda rocking in my chair."

"Anne looked toward me and smiled a tired looking smile. "Come on," I said. "It'll be fun. We'll swing by my room and get you a heavy coat and then go attack the hill."

"Why don't you just go?" she said.

"No, come on. Your paper is under control. You need to have some fun. It's the first snow. You only get one of these a year."

Anne smiled a weak smile and shook her head no, which meant OK. The shake was her way of reminding me that I always use some sort of trumped-up, grand lifetime perspective to convince her of things. You're only young once, I'd say. Or, someday you'll have responsibilities and won't be able to . . . .

Outside the world was muffled. There was no wind, and it didn't seem as cold. I could hear people yelling, but the sound didn't carry. It fell to the ground with the snow. Anne walked with me and held my hand, and for a while I forgot about our problem.

CHAPTER NINE

After Anne dropped out that Christmas, things changed between Jay and me. Our room wasn't party central any more. It was more like a sick room. My problem, of course, was Anne — or I should say the lack of Anne. I hadn't had a private talk with her since the day it snowed, the day I gave her my Merrill Lynch money.

Jay's problem was just as serious. His dad, a dentist, had been indicted for insurance fraud. They said he was beefing up his bills – charging for a root canal when he had only filled a cavity, I guess.

Jay's real trouble, besides the fact that his dad was facing jail time, was that Jay knew this overcharging business was his mom's fault. She had been doing his dad's books for years. And she was the one, Jay said, that had to drive a Jaguar and had to travel all over the world. Dr. Newton, Jay said, was not a flashy man and had no desire to be a millionaire. And as far as travel, he resented every second of vacation time he didn't spend at his fishing cabin on Lake Lanier, the big, rambling lake just north of Atlanta.

The thing that tore Jay up was that his dad was taking the entire heat on himself. And worse, his mom was letting it happen. Jay had to call his dad in the middle of the day at his office, because when he called home, his dad would make Jay talk to his mom, something he refused to do. Jay'd hang up when he heard her voice.

When this all first happened, it was the middle of January, and the weather was constantly grey and cold. Besides occasional meals, Jay rarely ever got out of bed. He just sat around thinking. No TV, no stereo, no nothing. He just laid in bed with a pillow over his face, waiting for his family to fall apart, or maybe cussing his dad for not letting things fall apart the way they should. Either way, he was wrapped up in his own problems and wasn't too interested in hearing me cry over Anne.

Before long, spring rush was starting, and there was some sort of party every night. I went to as many as I could. I was trying to get my mind off of Anne. Maybe I was half-heartedly looking for someone to replace her. But there was no one.

The one thing that interested Jay in the time after his dad's trouble started was reading the book *Will*, by G. Gordon Liddy, the ex-FBI agent who was mixed up in Watergate. Jay hadn't finished the third chapter by the time he started snuffing out cigarettes on the palm of his hand. It wasn't much later when he started going around the house challenging guys to a contest where you'd put a burning cigarette between each other's pressed-together forearms and see who pulled away first. At first, Jay would pull away, even though you could see by looking that he was trying his hardest not to. Then he started drinking bourbon straight from the bottle before his competitions, and he started winning every time — so much so that after a while, nobody, even the pledges, would play. After that, when he got tanked up, he'd just go around snuffing out butts on himself and insisting that he wasn't burnt, even though you could plainly see red marks. The more the guys said he was twisted, the more Jay seemed to like it.

All this time, his mom, who he still hadn't spoken to, kept sending him checks — big ones — three hundred, five hundred, and on his birthday, two thousand dollars. Jay didn't deposit them. But he didn't throw them away either. He just left them on the bar where the guys could see them. They had beer rings and ash smudges all over them. I kept telling him he better cash them before his mom changed her mind and had the bank stop payment, but Jay insisted he didn't need them, which was true, I guess, because except for trips to the liquor store, he hadn't left the house for a long time. No dates, no parties, no classes.

Then Jay made another move. The fraternity was doing its good deed for the term by collecting used clothing for the poor. And one basketball Saturday, when all the guys and their dates were at the house for a pre-gamer, Jay, already a couple Bloody Marys into the day, started making trips through the middle of the party with armfuls of his cloths — jeans, shirts, sweaters, suits, shoes — and dumping them into the dishwasher box we were using to collect the stuff. People just looked and laughed the first few trips he made, but as he kept coming, conversations ended and people watched. There was a Lou Reed tape playing. And damn if Jay didn't reappear with another armful of cloths and a stack of 4 or 5 ball caps on his head. He walked across the room without really looking at anyone, and dumped the stuff in the box. When he started back up the stairs, I followed him.

"Can you talk to me?" I asked.

"I can listen," he said."

"Jay, man, I'm not sure why you're doing this. I mean, damn." I followed him into our room. "If you're just putting on a show, we can go down after everybody leaves and get everything back. Maybe just leave a couple of sweaters, something like that."

He didn't say anything. He was emptying out his bottom drawer, including underwear.

"It's your stuff," I said, not able to think of any more logical argument. "You gotta get it back."

"Don't want it back," he said.

"Is this something to do with God? Giving to the poor? That kind of thing?" I said, mostly just trying to keep the conversation going. "You're not hearing voices, are you?"

"Only yours," he said.

"But are you listening? Can't you see I wanna help you?"

"You do help me," he said, and started out the door.

At the bottom of the stairs, everybody was still waiting and watching. Jay kept up the show, walking slowly, parting the crowd on the way to the big box, and tossing in his last armload. That was it. That was everything. . . , except for what he was wearing. And he even shucked off the Buchanan sweatshirt he was wearing and tossed it into the box, which was now full to the top. Wearing only a pair of grey sweat pants and an Easthampton High T-shirt, Jay walked over to the bar and started fixing himself another Bloody.

With Jay back at his old familiar post, and with the show over, the party started again and people went back to talking among themselves and drinking until it was almost time for tip-off. Then they filtered out of the house holding big cups of beer for the walk over. After they were gone it was just Jay and me.

I asked him if there was anything I could do, but he said no and then went up stairs to take a nap. I thought about calling his parents and telling them that their son was slipping over the edge. But then I thought it might be too much for him if they drove up from Atlanta and confronted him in his wrinkled gym cloths. Besides, I didn't owe them any courtesy. They were the ones screwing up their son's life. No, my main responsibility, my only responsibility, was to help Jay. Now that he was off his Liddy kick, at least he wasn't doing himself any physical harm. It was easy to see that he was awfully screwed up inside though, and I'll bet that hurt worse than any cigarette burn. I was sure he just felt lonely. And that was the symptom I was gonna try to treat.

CHAPTER TEN

The Thursday after all this happened, we had a mixer set with the KDs. I got home from a biology lab around 4:30 and decided to clean up our room in case the party wound its way up to the third floor. Sometimes they did, sometimes they didn't. It depended on whether the girls had done any pre-party drinking, and whether they felt comfortable with us, whether any of our guys were dating any of their girls. I know Kevin Stubbs went to the KD Christmas formal with a girl named Lynn, but I didn't know if they were still seeing each other. Anyway, I figured there was a good chance of having some visitors, and that was reason enough to get my boxers off the floor.

The weird thing was that Jay wasn't around. This was the first time in over a month he wasn't waiting for me when I got home. Another thing was that when I was downstairs wiping off the bar, I noticed the checks from his mom were missing. I had a crazy feeling that he was gone for good. I mean, his books were still on the shelf, but the place didn't smell like smoke, and of course his clothes were all gone.

I went down the hall and did some asking around. I found out he wasn't at lunch, and nobody had seen him all afternoon. I looked down into the parking lot and saw his truck was gone.

I finished tidying up. I made Jay's bed and then went down to a dinner of cold sandwiches. On mixer nights, nobody felt like doing dishes or hiking over to the dining hall. Then I went back to my room and worried.

At 6:30, the girls started arriving. The young ones, the pledges, arrived early in a big gang, wearing their sorority sweat shirts and their pledge pins, their khaki shorts and their Tretorn tennis shoes. They formed a circle around the keg on the front porch and kept to themselves. Then, later, the older girls started to show in groups of two or three. They wore jeans and topsiders and T-shirts from places like Hilton Head or Kiawah Island or Bermuda. Most of them wore their hair down around their shoulders. They walked straight into the house, laughing and screaming. The music started and with it, the party.

I was sitting in a rocking chair on the porch, watching the young ones stiffening their resolve to head inside. The sun was going down and the air was turning cold. There was still no sign of Jay. I watched the traffic, hoping to see his truck roll by. I played this little game I used to play when I was young and waiting for my mom to pick me up after school. OK, I said, Jay will be the twelfth car. Then I counted. Nothing. OK, nine more. Still nothing. I kept this up until dark. When I looked up, the young ones were inside, and I was alone. I filled up my beer and sat back down. I'd been to enough of these mixers to know that the party would eventually come to me, and I'd be glad to have the chair when it did. In the mean time, I just sat there.

I thought about the time Jay and I drove up to Sliding Rock, just on the other side of the North Carolina line. It wasn't a public park, but everybody knew about it. You had to park on the side of the road, down by this country store, and walk back into the woods, past a no trespassing sign, and down a long, beer-can-littered path. You could hear the rushing water before you got to the clearing and the rock.

Before I had my socks off, Jay was down to his shorts and flinging himself down the rock. It was like he didn't even consider the fact that he could bust his ass, or worse.

That was a real difference between Jay and me. He trusted the obvious. I mean, judging by all the beer bottles, it's clear that hundreds of thrill seekers had put themselves at the mercy of the rock and lived to laugh about it. If there had been more than a couple of deaths, there would have been a barbed wire fence around the place. There wasn't.

I doubt Jay thought it through this way, but I think in his own short-hand way, that's what he was doing — trusting the obvious. I did, I do, think that way, but the obvious conclusion — go for it — did not convince me. I had to size it up for myself, like I was the first pilgrim to dip my feet in that cold mountain water. Jay rode and rode until he was whipped from scrambling back up the rocks. I went down once, and bumped my head pretty hard when I landed. I was lucky. Jay was immune.

So I was sitting in the rocking chair, picturing Jay lying face down in the shallow pool at the bottom of the sliding rock, wearing that same pair of sweat pants, with night falling. I was worrying the way a parent must worry, the way my mom must have worried when I was out too late or away on a trip. I realized I was worrying as much for myself as for Jay — like what would happen to me if something happened to him? How would it affect me? I guess that's natural. I guess that when you care for someone, you open yourself up to a world of possible pain. Because things end, even if it isn't your doing. People die. People change. And you're left just standing there. Sometimes just thinking the wrong thing is enough. Sometimes something makes people change — that's Anne. I believe, I know, Anne loved me. The abortion must have been just too much for her, like locking the door on someone you hoped would visit. I don't blame her for that, but I'd change it if I could. I don't know why God puts that voice in your head telling you to have sex with someone you love when it leads to so much trouble. I'm not done loving Anne. I'm not done with Jay yet either. I at least have to see him through this mess. Jay, where are you?

After a while, a girl I knew from my Political Science class came out onto the porch, and we talked about the term papers we had to write. Her hair was dark and fell over her shoulders. It looked something like Anne's, but not really. I bored her for a while talking about the Teapot Dome Scandal and then she went back inside. I filled my beer again and then sat back down. There was still no sign of Jay. I figured he must have gone to Atlanta. Maybe something happened with his dad? But I knew his court date wasn't here yet. Maybe his sister was having some trouble? I knew this thing was hard on all of them, but I also knew that his sister was at home with his mom, and unless something had changed, Jay had no intention of going anywhere near there. And what about the checks? If he was just going home, what would he need with four or five thousand dollars?

The beer was making me feel a little tired, so I put my head back and closed my eyes for a while. I nearly swallowed my tongue when my chair fell backward. I braced to hit the floor. But I didn't. I stopped in mid-timber. I looked up and saw Jay's upside down face, straining as he held me up.

"Pick me up, wise ass," I said.

He did, and then picked up a bottle of Jim Beam that was missing only a couple of swigs. He plopped down in the chair next to me and kicked his feet up on the rail. He had a haircut and a shave. He wore a black Polo sports shirt and a pair of khaki trousers with a stiff, sharp crease running down to a pair of shiny black penny loafers slipped over blue socks with a crisscross golf club pattern.

"Been shopping, Huh?" I said.

"You could say that."

"I guess you sorta needed a few things."

"Got more than a few things," he said. "Here, have a shot and then help me unload."

I took a pretty big pull — I was already half lit — and then followed him around the house to his truck. He opened the passenger-side door, and an avalanche of boxes and bags fell onto the gravel.

"Jesus," I said. "You opening your own store?"

"Man needs to watch his appearance. The ladies don't want to date a bum."

I laughed, grateful to have him back, and loaded my arms full of the fashion equivalent of his mom's bribe checks. As I followed him up the stairs, I tried to figure out whether this was a good or a bad sign. Was he out of his funk and ready to rejoin the living, or was this just one more step on the way to the asylum? I didn't know, but at least he was smiling and interested. That was the Jay I knew. That was the Jay I missed.

I'm not sure why this happened — or at least I hate to think this is how things work — but the day after Jay got all his new cloths, girls started hovering around. Good-looking girls. Juniors and seniors. Girls we never even thought of dating. Somehow, with these new clothes Jay went from being just one of the guys to being Mr. Smooth. It's not that his personality changed really. He was the same old Jay, the same funny accent, the same sense of humor. He was just pumped. He had energy, enthusiasm. You could see it in his face. You could hear it in his voice. He was that way with everyone, including me. For the first time in months he was interested in me. How's my family? How are my classes going? How do I feel about Anne these days? Am I gonna try to get her back? Am I gonna forget about her? Can he help me?

At first, I was happy to see Jay back in action. But the more I watched him, the more I thought he was bending in a different direction. All the dates, all the attention he was getting, didn't seem to satisfy him. He was never relaxed. He never stopped. He was working, working, working. He seemed to be chasing something he couldn't see.

CHAPTER ELEVEN

Jay woke me at four a.m. on the morning of his Dad's sentencing. He was already dressed in his new double-breasted Brooks Brother's blazer. His hair was wet combed. A cigarette hung between his lips.

"Jimmy, I gotta be with my dad today," he said, putting a big Styrofoam cup of coffee in my hand. "Please come with me. I need you there."

I was awake, and not groggy like usual. I felt like I used to feel when my Dad would wake me to go fishing. Somehow your head is very clear when you're up before the sun. Everything seemed simple. I borrowed one of Jay's starched shirts and a tie, and then threw on a pair of khakis and my blue blazer. We were out the door, in his pick-up, and rolling through the dark down I-85 before I finished my coffee.

As I watched him drive, I realized that it was the first time I had seen him worry since he's gone shopping. I spoke up after a while.

"You think he's going to jail? I said.

"Don't know. Sure as hell hope not," he said, taking his eyes off the road and looking at me for a second. "Hopefully he'll just get fined. Least that way the guilty will be punished along with the innocent."

"I don't know," I said after a while. "I doubt your mom would enjoy seeing your Dad go to the slammer."

"Yea, I guess the ladies at the club would talk."

"Listen, don't you think it's time you ease up on her? It's not as simple as you're making it out. How long have your folks been married?"

"I don't know, 20 or so."

"Don't you think your mom would have walked a long time ago if all she was interested in was money? I'll give you the fact that she was stupid to mess with Uncle Sam, but I can't believe she did it to make your dad suffer."

"But that's how it came out."

"Yea, but by that time it was too late for her to do anything about it."

"That's the point," he said. "She could have done something. She can do something. She could tell the truth."

"You ever think maybe she just doesn't have it in her? I mean you gotta believe she's scared as hell. Just because she's your mom doesn't mean she doesn't feel alone and scared. Look at it this way: Your dad has a lot of guts. He's putting himself on the line to protect your family. He's a damn hero, and one per family is more than your share. Don't you think he's already forgiven your mom? All you need to do is let him carry out his plan. Let him be a hero. I mean, there's nothing you can do to help him. The least you can do is not screw up something he's risking himself to achieve. He's doing what he's doing for you as much as for your mom."

That was all the talking for a while. Jay just watched the road. I put my head back and closed my eyes, but I couldn't sleep.

I didn't know whether Jay was pissed at me for taking his mom's side. Maybe he was just thinking about what I said. I was kinda surprised I came up with that hero stuff. It wasn't planned. But the more I thought about it, the more sense it made. The best thing for all of them would be to get past the crisis and get things back to normal. I know that's what Jay wanted, even if he didn't know it.

Just after sun-up we crossed the state line into Georgia. We passed over Lake Hartwell — wide and green with red clay banks. There was a big sign for a restaurant and gas station called Dad's, which marked the turn off for a lake house we used to visit on retreats. But we rushed right past it. We were two hours from Atlanta.

It was almost 9:00 by the time we pushed through the rush-hour traffic and made it to the Federal Court building. We pulled over to the side of the street. Jay grabbed his jacket and got out. I slid over to the driver's side and drove off to find a parking space."

I finally found a garage that would take the pick-up. It was about ten blocks from the courthouse, and it cost me six of the ten bucks I had in my pocket. As I walked back, I thought about how much I hated Atlanta. Anne was somewhere in the city, hiding from me. And every one of the people on the street — the men in suits, the people in the shops, the men driving delivery trucks — every one of them, no matter how nice they acted, no matter how they smiled or howdyed you or told you to have a good day, they were all helping her. The traffic cops and the one-way streets and the big glass buildings, they all formed a wall between me and her. Apart from Jay, I didn't have an ally in the whole damn ant farm.

I got back to the courthouse. It was almost 10:00. I walked up the granite steps, through the heavy door, and into the cool, dark lobby. I could hear the clap of my footsteps echo off the walls as I walked up to the guard and asked him which room the sentencing was in. He sent me down a long hall.

When I got to room C-1124, I thought for the first time that I didn't have any business going inside. I didn't think Dr. Newton would want me in there. Nobody but Jay knew how much I knew about this whole thing. And it's not the kind of thing you want to advertise.

I looked through the little window in the door and saw Dr. Newton leaning over the front pew, talking to Jay's mom and sister. Jay and his little brother were standing off to the side with their hands in their pockets. There was no judge on the bench, only a lady off to the side packing her court reporter typewriter into its case. The family looked serious, but they weren't crying or anything. I backed away before any of them saw me and walked back to the lobby and out onto the outside steps.

It was growing into a nice spring day. The sky was a deep clear blue, and a cool breeze stirred the treetops. It seemed like a good day to get off easy. I hoped the judge thought so. When Dr. Newton walked out that door, the hard part would either be over or just beginning.

It wasn't long before the courthouse door swung open and Jay and his brother, Phillip, walked out. Jay gave me a little up and down nod, which told me that things had gone OK inside. Whether that meant no jail I didn't know. The guys passed me and went down to the bottom of the steps. Jay lit a cigarette and they waited.

Then Dr. Newton and Jay's sister, Martha, walked out holding hands. Jay's mom was following them. Martha was sniffling and wiping her eyes, but I figured it was for some childish reason. Maybe the judge scared her. Maybe it was just being in that cold, hollow building. I doubted she was crying over a fine. But Dr. Newton held on to her, and she was drying up. Dr. Newton himself seemed fine. He wasn't smiling, but he didn't look worried either.

Then all five of them were together in front of the courthouse, standing in the sunshine. And I was sitting up above them, watching a family get back together, feeling the pressure blow away in the cool breeze, knowing that I was witnessing the end of a bad episode.

Before I knew it, they were smiling. Dr. Newton was holding Jay's mom's hand in a way I guessed they hadn't done in a long time. From up on top of the steps, I was sharing the sweet, mixed sadness of something lost and something more important gained. I wanted to go down there. I wanted to be part of it. But that same something told me that I owed it to them to keep my distance.

I thought about my own family — so organized, so smooth, undisturbed, unchallenged, almost crying out for a crisis and then a recommitment. But it wasn't the right time for that. It was my time to break away and learn to be myself. Then I could come back a different and better person. That's what college is for. Geology and geometry are just side notes, something to do while you go through the long process of painting your self-portrait.

After a while Dr. Newton started looking at his watch. Jay shifted on his feet. They were getting ready to say good-bye. Dr. Newton stuck out his hand and Jay shook it and smiled. Then Mrs. Newton stepped up, and Jay gave her a little kiss on the cheek. Jay started to back away, but she put her arms around him and hugged. When it was over, Jay gave his brother a pat on the back and then started up the steps toward me. They all looked up at me. I stood up and waved. They waved and then walked away.

"So?" I said when Jay got close.

"Hundred and Eighty thousand plus probation," he said.

"Not bad. Not bad."

"Yeah," he said. "Not bad."

CHAPTER TWELVE

After the sentencing, Jay was feeling pretty upbeat. We drove up to a place called the Varsity, just across from Georgia Tech, one of his old hangouts. We sat in a Formica booth and ate grilled cheese sandwiches and onion rings and drank sweet iced tea. He was talking a lot about his high school days. He told me again how his football team, the Easthampton Hornets, beat the Pace Panthers his senior year and how he got to ring the victory bell, the school's top sporting honor. "We got the bell. Panthers go to hell."

Soon the conversation wound around to Anne. From the way Jay talked, it was easy to see that she was a big part of his life in high school. He told me he didn't know why, but he never wanted to date her. He said he liked her too much to take a chance on ruining their friendship. I thought that was crap. What guy could spend any time with Anne without falling in love? The reason they never dated was probably because she always had someone else on the hook. But that doesn't explain what happened last year at Buchanan. After she cut that lawyer loose, Jay was right there. He was seeing that girl Kelly, the one from Charleston, but that was nothing and Anne knew it. And yet she picked me. As far as I could see, I didn't have any thing on Jay. We were both just regular guys. But somehow Anne didn't think so. She saw something in me that I guess was there all along. I wanted to be in love, I wanted to give a girl my love and do it right, I mean, not take advantage. And she saw that. At least she saw it at the time. I didn't know how she felt now.

After lunch we bought a six-pack of Bud tall boys and drove over to Easthampton High. We jumped the fence at the football stadium and climbed to the top of the concrete stands. A thunderstorm was stirring up in the western sky and the air fell still and quiet the way it does before a hard rain.

A grey haired man dressed in a drab janitor's uniform was out pushing one of those machines that make chalk lines on the field. He kept looking over his shoulder at the gathering storm. Thunder started to rumble. He stood still for a second and then gave up and pushed the machine up under the stands.

I was feeling a little drunk, and my head was full of Anne. I was stuck. There was no way around it. I had to see her. I had to explain. I didn't know what I'd say. I didn't know what I'd done really. I was only trying to help, trying to do what was best for both of us.

Jay was staring at the bell at the top of the tower in the endzone. He looked at it hard. Then he stood up and started bounding down the stands, beer sloshing out of his can. When he got to the bottom, he jumped the little fence and crossed over the running track and ran out onto the field. Then he went to the fifty-yard line and hunched down in a three-point stance. The air was dark and heavy and still, and I could hear him calling signals — "38. 38. Hup. Hup." And he was off, running in a wide arch, swinging out toward the far sideline, looking over shoulder for the invisible pass. He stuck his hands out for catch and then cradled the two-year-old memory in his right forearm and hauled it into the end zone and beyond. Then in a leap he was on the ladder, climbing toward the bell. I stood and smiled as he scrambled up the rungs. boNG. boNG. D-DONG. The sound of victory echoed off the visitor's stands and rolled out over the red-brick campus.

The rain was coming, and I felt like this was Jay's last crazy act. He was cured.

By the time we made it back to the truck we were both pretty well soaked. Jay was laughing and that rubbed off on me a little bit, but not enough to distract me from my main business. We took our ties off and hung them over the rear view mirror. Jay asked what I wanted to do now. I just looked at him, and he started the truck, and we set off toward Anne's house.

The rain slowed to a drizzle as we drove along the dogwood-lined street through neighborhoods filled with big brick homes with circular driveways and blooming azalea bushes. Soon, we pulled into a development with a sign at the entrance that said Pierce Mills. It looked a lot like all the other neighborhoods we had passed with its rows of newly built brick homes and its manicured lawns. At the end of the street we took a left and then drove past a few more houses and up to the McGowen's. Jay pulled the truck in behind a long grey Buick.

We smoothed our shirts and combed our hair. I had a feeling she was watching me. I could feel her eyes on me, and I had trouble drawing a breath. I grabbed Jay's pack of Marlboro Lights and sparked one. My hands shook.

"You OK," Jay asked.
"Yea, I guess. I don't know."
"Want me to go in and see if she's around?"
"Would you mind?"
"Hell no — after all you've done for me today?"

He was out the door, and he jogged up the driveway through the drizzle and up under the covered walk connecting the garage with the house. He knocked on the kitchen door, and after a second it opened and he went in. My cigarette was still burning, but I'd forgotten to take a drag. I put it out and waited.

I was still jumpy. I felt like she was gonna walk out the kitchen door any second and come up and ask me what the hell I was doing bothering her. I didn't know how I was going to be able to say what I needed to say there in the driveway. What I needed was some time with her, some privacy. It could take me hours to come up with just the right words.

After some time, the front door opened and Jay walked out — alone.

From his face, I couldn't tell what had happened. He looked blank — not happy, not worried, not anything. He climbed into the truck and started it up.

"She wasn't there?" I said.

He pulled the truck out onto the road and we started out of the neighborhood.

"Was she there?" I asked again.

"Jimmy, she doesn't want to see you."

"Huh? Why not? I mean . . . what's . . ."

"I'm sorry man, but it's just that simple. She won't see you. She made me promise I'd just get in the truck and drive you back to school. She's OK. She's not sick or anything. She just doesn't want to face you. I guess she just doesn't think it'd be a good time . . . ah . . . Listen, I don't know, that's just a guess. I don't know what she's thinking. All I know is what she told me."

We got to the entrance of the neighborhood, the stop sign, and Jay rolled the truck to a stop. I turned around to see if there was anyone behind us. There wasn't. I unbuckled my seat belt and looked at Jay. He was staring straight ahead. He wouldn't look at me.

Before I decided for sure what I was gonna do, I was out the door and running through the wet grass. Jay threw the truck into reverse, propped his arm up on the seat, and started backing down the street after me. The transmission whined.

He was yelling something, but I couldn't hear. The leather soles of my loafers were sliding on the grass, so I kicked them off and kept running in my socks. I tried to cut behind the house on the corner, but when I got around the garage, I came to a tall redwood fence. I wheeled around and ran back around the garage.

When I got back to the front, Jay's truck was parked and he was standing in the center of the lawn, his arms out.

"Slow down now, buddy. It's OK. OK."

I stopped and looked at him, panting. There was no oxygen in my whole body, and I had a cramp in my belly that hurt like hell.

When my lungs filled up enough so I could speak, I told him to get out of my way. But he stood there like a linebacker ready to throw a body block.

"Just leave me alone," I said. "This isn't your business."

"Calm down now. It's OK."

He said it was OK, but he was still standing there, set, like he wanted to throw me for a loss. I relaxed, went loose, but when Jay did the same, lowering his hands and standing up straight, I bolted.

He chased me. In my socks, I was faster, but he was right behind me. I went around the house on the corner, and down toward Anne's house. As I circled around a hedge, Jay jumped over it and made a dive for my feet. He missed, and I left him sprawled out in the wet grass in his new Brooks Brothers suit pants.

I got to her front door and banged on it with my fist. Then I felt Jay grab me from behind. I spun around and pushed him away.

"Why are you chasing me?" I yelled. "What in the world are you doing? I thought you wanted to help me."

"I do," he said. "I did. I . . ."

"What? You what?"

"She told me . . . She asked me . . ."

"WHAT?"

He looked at me for a second, and then the air went out of him. His shoulders dropped. "Nothing," he said. "Nothing. Do what you like. I'm with you. It's just not worth it."

Then I heard her voice. She said my name. I looked around, but I couldn't see her. Then I looked up. There she was. She was looking down at me from a second story window. I was off balance. Her face wasn't the same. It wasn't the picture I had been carrying around in my mind since before Christmas. Her hair was gone. Her long beautiful black hair was trimmed up to her ears. And her face was round and red. I couldn't tell if she was the girl I loved or not, I was so used to loving her memory.

"Anne," I said. "I need to see you. I need to talk to you."

"Jimmy, Please just go away. Please. I don't want to talk to you. I don't was to see you. There's no use. It's all different now. It's all changed. Greer and I are back together. We're getting married."

I looked at Jay sitting down on the stoop. I sat down next to him. When I looked back up, Anne was gone and the window was closed. After a while, I tried the front door, but it was locked.

CHAPTER THIRTEEN

Three days after our trip to Atlanta, the second Friday in May, it was time to get back in the car and head for the beach. Jay, who had seemed preoccupied since his dad's sentencing, had already made arrangements to drive down with this tennis player he'd been seeing named Pam, and there was really only room for two in his pick-up. So I drove down with Ted Cross, a senior from Pennsylvania, and a couple of little sisters we'd been paired up with since neither Ted nor I had asked a real date.

Ted was engaged to a girl who went to Rutgers, his old high school girlfriend. On the long drive down, the girls stayed mostly to themselves except for a little polite conversation, and Ted and I shot the shit mostly about how weird the idea of getting married seemed, the idea of spending the rest of your life with the same girl. We also talked about the job offer he had from Proctor & Gamble. From what he said, it sounded like he was going to drive around from one grocery store to the next making sure his soap and deodorant was shelved at a housewife's eye level. It sounded kinda dull, but he seemed excited, so I kept my opinion to myself. "Sales are where the money is," he said, gleaming.

The whole way down Interstates 26, you saw cars filled with college kids, smiling and laughing and tapping their fingers on dashboards in time with whatever was on their tape deck. The highway was also lousy with state troopers picking off speeders as fast as they could write tickets. Every mile or so you'd see flashing blues and cars pulled over and licenses being checked and beers being poured out onto the hot pavement. But even with that it was hard to slow down. It was the kind of day that made you ache to have your feet wet or covered in sand and made you cuss every minute and every mile that stood between you and where you wanted to be.

A part of the excitement even got to me, even though I was still reeling from seeing Anne and the whole weekend sorta snuck up on me. Whatever else was happening, one thing I never completely soured on was the fun of a good party, the feeling of letting all your worries go and being swallowed up by the crowd and the music and the sweat, but above all the feeling of being known and being able to move in any direction and seeing and talking to people who liked you and accepted you as one of their own. You can find the music and the beer and the crowds anywhere, but even if you're lucky there will never be more than two or three places where you're a true insider, and that even passes because the scene changes and the people move on. It's as much about time as it is place.

Below Columbia, we, along with almost every other car on the highway, exited and took Interstate 20 up toward Florence. Every mile the traffic stacked up more. Once we got through the city, the road narrowed to two lanes and the congestion was to the point where you couldn't get going faster than around forty. The road was straight and boring and the only thing to look at were new-growth pine trees for the paper mills. Then, finally, we started to see billboards for golf courses and factory outlets and hotels. Then the signs got thicker and there were a few sorry shacks and a place you could buy hubcaps. Then the trees thinned out and we went around a bend and saw an interchange with a big green sign showing the way to North Myrtle Beach and Cherry Grove. I took the exit and drove over the bridge and down a feeder road for a few miles. Then, suddenly, we were at the beach. The sun was shining, though it was dipping low, there was a lot of traffic, and the parking lots in front of the restaurants and grocery stores were overflowing. Up the street on the left there was an amusement park with a pool-water blue water slide rising up over the trees. A party store on the right had a big inflatable Bud Man — like a float from a Macy's parade — standing on the roof. Tom, who had fallen asleep, perked back up and rooted in the cooler for two cold beers and cracked one for me.

After a few wrong turns, we made it to the strip — Ocean Drive — and it was clear the weekend was already in high gear. All the hotels and guesthouses had fraternity and sorority banners hanging from them. Girls walked along the road in bikinis and bare feet. Guys hung from the back of pick-up trucks, hooting. Loud, distorted rock and roll blasted from a hundred different sources, mixing in the air. The sun was going down."

Finally, I spotted our hotel. The Oceanaire. The lot was already full, but I was beat from the trip and didn't feel like cruising around for a space, so I parked behind Jay's truck. We got out of the car. The place was a zoo. A John Prine tape was blasting, and a bunch of guys were in the pool playing water polo with an empty keg. Some others were wrestling in the grass, some were playing paddleball, and some were playing shuffle board, trying to keep mugs of beer balanced on the disks. A drunk Olympics.

Marty was over by the kegs. He saw me and nodded and walked over.

"I see the gentlemen's engines have been started," I said.

"Been like this all afternoon," Marty said. "I don't know where the bastards get the energy."

I turned around and the girls had already disappeared. Ted was over on the seawall checking out the ocean.

"What kept you," he said. "Way I remember it, you and I cracked the first keg together last year."

"Yea, well I actually went to class this morning."

"Y'musta been the only one."

"Damn near."

"Score some good brownie points?"

"You know me. That's how I keep my grades in the stratosphere."

We stood and watched the crowd for a second. Then I asked if he'd seen Jay.

"He was around before," Marty said. "He's probably over at Crazy Zack's with the rest of the world."

I left Marty and walked into the lobby where I found Jay's and my name on a list and a key corresponding to our room number hanging on a rack of unpainted plywood and nails. Upstairs, I let myself in and found that Jay had already settled in. The bed nearest the window was rumpled and there was a damp bathing suit and T-shirt in the sink. On the cloths rack hung several of his new shirts and pairs of trousers, each piece professionally laundered and starched and wrapped in its own clear plastic bag. I turned on the news and listened while I unpacked.

I thought about the year before, how Anne and I had worked it out so we could have a room together, and how she unpacked so neatly, putting her cloths in the drawers and in the closet and setting her makeup and curlers and blow dryer on the table by the sink. We both knew it was going to be the first time we were going to sleep together, and she made it all very nice for me, very grown up feeling.

After a while I drew back the drapes and looked out. It was dark and the beer athletes had gone. The ocean had disappeared.

There were just a few guys in sight, standing over by the kegs. When the news was over, there was no sign of Jay, so I dressed and swung down by Marty's room. I knocked, but he wasn't around, so I walked down to the seawall and listened to the ocean and felt the salt breeze wash over me.

I wandered over and talked to the keg boys, but they were all exhausted and sunburnt and somewhere far south of drunk. I drew a beer and then slipped away and start walking toward Zack's.

At its simplest, Crazy Zack's was nothing special. It was just another big bar on Ocean Drive, a sprawling, low slung wooden building surrounded by a pitted marl parking lot that held grey puddles when it rained. Inside it was just a big, dim room with wooden walls and wooden floors and a long wooden bar that stretched the length of one whole wall. It was a place for beer and beach music, shagging music, dancing music, pretty much like every other bar along the grand strand. But that doesn't even start to cover it.

At the time, Zack's was everything. If you went to college in the Carolinas or Virginia, or even high school, if you planned to be a stockbroker some day, or a doctor, or a lawyer or schoolteacher, if you were gonna be married some day and have kids and a house and a lawn, if you bought your cloths from L.L. Bean and Brooks Brothers, if you were young and white and had a little money in your pocket, then Zach's was the edge, the place you had to be.

The spring before, Anne and I could not get enough of the place. We were there till closing on Thursday, Friday and Saturday night — holding hands, drinking beer from plastic cups the size of paint cans, dancing barefooted on the sticky wooden floor.

But this spring Anne was gone, and when I got close enough, I saw that place was packed, and that there was a line around the parking lot long enough to fill the place again. I stood across the street and watched for a while and listened to the music escaping over the side porch wall.

Then I turned and headed back to the Oceanaire and back to my room.

Figuring I'd wait for the bars to close and the party to come back to me, I switched the TV on and took a nap that ended up lasting all night.

I woke up to the sound of Jay fumbling with his key in the door lock. He let himself in, and the morning light pushed in behind him and filled the room. I still had my street cloths on, and I was sleeping on top of the covers. The only part of the bed unmade was the pillows, and I was resting on one and hugging the other. I didn't stir when Jay walked in so he didn't know if I was awake. Without closing the door, he walked across the room to the sink and dropped his pants and pulled on his swimming trunks. When I said good morning, he turned and looked at me with eyes that told me his brain was still in low gear.

"Rough night?" I said.

"Not too, but kinda late," he said. "Think I'm gonna go catch a nap on the beach."

I sat up and stretched and looked at my watch. It was 8:15.

"You crash with Pam?" I asked.

"Naa. We kinda lost each other at Zack's."

"I'm sorry."

"It's no problem," he said, grabbing a towel and walking out the door. "I got her right where I want her."

I sat there and thought about his right-where-I-want-her remark and decided it was just talk. Then Jay stuck his head back in the door and said, "See you down there in a little while?" I nodded, and he pulled the door shut, and the room was dark again.

I layed back and dozed for another hour or so until the big stereo started cranking Robert Gordon's version of *It's Only Make Believe*, and the splashing and hooting started down at the pool. I put on some shorts and a T-shirt and went out on to the porch and let the sun bake me awake. The day was already hot. The sky was pale blue and low hanging above and hazy at the horizon. The ocean was calm and grey. Small, unenthusiastic waves rolled onto the apron of the wide, hard-packed shore, already decorated with an odd patchwork of blankets and towels and studded with red-fleshed, motionless sunbathers. Above the seawall, the grass was covered with another rank of sunbathers, and closer, the pool stirred with laughing and splashing and Nerf-ball-throwing swimmers.

I stood three floors up, surveying the scene and wondering what to do with myself. Tradition dictated a Wiffle-baseball game, so I figured I'd get that going.

I found the ball and bat in the bed of Jay's pick-up. And as I walked out through the sunbathers and down onto the sand, with a few nods and a little eye contact and a few dramatic swings of the bat, I gathered enough guys to start an informal game. And after a few minutes of warming up and a few heroic outfielder catches at the shoreline, we'd attracted enough guys for a full-blown, eighteen man game.

After a little more warming up and deciding on teams, the game started, and before long I was absorbed into the action. Buzzed by the sun and dripping sweat, everything that had happened to me since I'd played the same game the year before, everything that had been occupying my mind, melted away, and for a while I was that same brain-dead freshman again, smiling and laughing easily and walking like a giant.

After a couple of hours of playing, I split off with a few other guys, and we took a long walk along the boardwalk, checking out the girls and watching the pelicans fly in formation overhead, floating on the hot air rising off the sand.

When we got back near the Oceanaire, we could see there was a strange lack of activity on our beach. As we got closer, we could see that up near the pool there was a silent crown circled around a table. Jay was among the people standing, so I walked up beside him. I stood on my toes and discovered there was a poker game in progress. Marty was among the players, along with five other deadly serious looking seniors.

"There's around a thousand bucks on the table," Jay said.

"Jesus."

They were playing a game I knew. It's called acey-deucy or high-low. The dealer shows you two cards, and you bet on whether the next card will be higher than one and lower than the other. The twist to the game is that if the third card matches either of the first two cards, the player has to pay twice his bet into the pot. That's what was happening here, but it was out of control. Apparently, every time someone bet the pot (which was the only way to end the game), a match came up. And now the pot was too big to take a chance on loosing. So it kept growing.

It was clear no one sat down to a nickel-dime-quarter game thinking they were going to win or loose hundreds of dollars. No one had that much to loose. The chits on the table amounted to more-that most of these guys had in their checking accounts back at school. But there was no easy way out."

The dealer was a guy named Peter Ambrosini, last year's fraternity vice-president, and he suspended his dealing and argued that they should just stop the game and everybody take there money back and just forget about it. That drew nods of approval from the gallery.

But Marty wouldn't hear it. He said the players had been paying in and winning back chunks of money for over an hour, and that he was down over a hundred dollars in addition to what he had in the pot, and that there was no good way to back out.

"I don't mean to be an asshole here," Marty said, "but when you take a seat at the table, you play till the game's over."

I could see a couple of the players getting red-faced. And the folks watching looked at each other with eyes that asked why

Marty was insisting on pushing forward with a thing that was so clearly out of hand."

I tried to figure Marty's angle. I didn't think it was the hundred bucks he was out or the chance of winning the pile in the middle of the table. I wondered if it was something about honor, or its weaker cousin, saving face. But I decided it was simpler than all that. I figured Marty just wanted to see the game end the way it started — among friends. Loosing money on the turn of a card was one thing. You could only blame the cards, or yourself. But loosing or winning on the basis of fear, on the showing of hands, even if unanimous, is wrong. No one would be satisfied, and you could never have a serious game again. That must have been what he was thinking.

So after some time and a few sweaty smiles and a few tentative pulls at a tequila bottle, Pete shuffled and started to deal again. And the folks all watched.

The players were all waiting for a sure thing — an ace/two, or at least an ace/three or king/two. And the game went around the table again. Finally, from somewhere toward the bottom of the deck, the ace/three appeared. The rhythm broke. And the two cards stared up at Marty. Everyone sat there and waited to see what he would do.

Marty reached into the center of the table and had a look at the chits, reminding himself of what was at stake. One of the guys asked him how much was in there, and Marty said it was a little over eleven hundred.

Pete started to launch back into his argument on why they should stop the game, but Marty held a hand up, and Pete fell silent.

Then Marty stiffened his face and said, "Let's get this over with. I bet it all. Pot."

Pete held the remnants of the deck in his hand, and he carefully peeled a single card from the top and placed it between the ace and three that were already there. The new card was a three.

Marty stared at the cards for a moment with a kind of resigned look on his face. Some of the folks walked back toward the beach, not wanting to be around if there was trouble. But Marty didn't bitch. He didn't say anything. He just took up a pencil and ripped a corner of paper from his note pad and filled in another IOU. Then he pushed it into the pot.

Pete didn't speak either. Instead he raked together the cards and reunited the deck and placed it neatly on the table in front of him. Then he reached over and collected up all the chits as if to have a look, but instead he crumpled them in his hand and dropped them to the ground and walked away.

Marty didn't wait too long until he stood and walked away too.

After the game ended and the crown dispersed, I stayed by the pool and realized that the enthusiasm I felt during the ball game and my hike along the board walk had disappeared. I was back where I started — nursing my bad luck.

The sun was edging down toward the top of the hotel, and the die-hard sunbathers were giving up one by one. Jay came by the lawn chair I was sitting in and asked if I wanted to join a gang that was driving up to the North Carolina state line for a Calabash seafood dinner. I told him thanks but no thanks. I bummed a couple of cigarettes from him and then watched him walk up toward the room. I sat and smoked.

An hour or so later, I was still there, sitting at the edge of the pool with my feet dangling in the water. I watched the light come on in all the rooms, and I watched the girls with curlers in their hair hurrying from room to room with extra sweaters and shoes — comparing.

Then, from the room closest to the pool, I heard someone yell, "Enough." It was Marty and Pete's room. Marty walked out with his saddlebags packed and slung over his shoulder. His motorcycle was waiting over by the battery of empty kegs. He walked over and slung the bags over the black leather seat. He looked up and saw me watching him. He walked over toward me, leaned over and put his hand in the pool and wiped the water on his face.

"You're not leaving," I said.

"I thought I'd get an early start. I've got a paper due on Tuesday."

"Yeah." I knew about the paper. Everybody did. It was his senior seminar paper — the one he didn't quite get to last semester, or the one before.

"If you gotta, you gotta."

"Yeah, well, I gotta."

"Listen, you're not pissed about the poker game, are you? I mean, it was just something that happened. It wasn't anybody's fault."

"A thing doesn't have to be somebody's fault to be upsetting.

"Yeah, well, I guess you're right. But still, we only get two days a year down here. I hate to see you have to cut it short."

"Jimmy, I just can't hang with the fraternity any more. Most of the guys, and shit, all the girls feel like the world owes them something, like just because their parents drive a Mercedes and have ten thousand bucks a year to send them to Buchanan, their way is clear. But there's a lot of things they don't know, a lot they don't consider when they make their little plans."

"Like what?"

"Aw, you know, Jim. You're a smart guy. You ain't part of this preppy fantasy. I knew that the first time I met you. You knew more about being a human being when you were a freshman than most of these dumbasses know when they're seniors, more than they'll ever know."

"Man, that's news to me. I barely feel like I know which way is up."

"That's just it. You know enough to say you don't know anything. You think most of these guys would admit that? Hell no. They have all the answers. They've got their lives all planned out.

They quit asking questions in the sixth grade. All they want is their parent's lives — their parent's lives plus ten percent more, to show the world's making progress. That's bullshit, Jimmy. You know that. The answer is that there are no answers. Only questions."

I sat there and watched my legs in the blue, lighted water, my shins pale and angling off at the surface. A gang of girls were dancing and milling around on the balcony. From inside a room with an open door, one of the guys let out a big war whoop, a big YEE-HAW, and some of the guys cheered.

"Why do they seem so damn happy?" I said.

"They are, buddy."

I sat there a second. "Man, I don't need to hear this."

Marty laughed and put his hand on my shoulder. "You'll be OK, Jimmy."

He walked back over to his bike, kicked it over, put on his helmet, gassed it and was gone.

After that, I sat for a while and then walked over to the arcade and shot some pool. When I walked back outside an hour later, the sun had gone down. I went back to my room and pulled on a sweater my mom had picked up for me in Scotland and wrapped a blue bandanna around my head the way Marty did to keep his helmet from rubbing his forehead. I didn't bother with shoes. From my balcony, I could hear the music from Zack's. I decided to head over.

When I got there, the place was overflowing. There was a line at the door, and you had to wait for someone to go out before you could go in. I was alone, so I got in quick. As soon as my eyes adjusted, I could see a hundred people I knew."

Zack's didn't feel like Zack's without Anne. There were girls there with dark, shiny hair like Anne's, girls with turtlenecks and sweaters and Levis and Bermuda shorts, all of which could have come from Anne's closet, but none of them was Anne. I could love any one of them, I thought. I mean, what's the big difference? It's not like Anne was the only girl on the beach. But I didn't love any of them, and that's the thing about love.

I thought of a documentary I saw on T.V. about this island where sea gulls went to breed. At the height of the season there were hundreds of thousands of identical looking gulls, one right next to the other. But yet, when the mama bird flew off and plucked an anchovy from the ocean, she knew just which chick to bring it back to. I don't know how that kind of thing works, but I know that's how it goes.

And that homing instinct didn't only apply to me. I barely had time to get a bucket of beer and station myself at the rail that overlooked the dance floor, when two soft slender hands reached around from behind me and covered my eyes. I didn't need to guess. I knew it was Ginny. I turned around and she was on me — kissing me, hugging me, pushing her leg in between mine, spilling half my beer. She was drunk and energetic.

"Dance with me, please," she said.

I thought of Anne. I wished the hands, the lips on me were hers. But here was Ginny. That was the fact — a fact I guessed I could live with. I chugged the beer left in my cup, and she took my hand, and we pushed out on to the dance floor. Ginny looked over at her girlfriends, who were watching our every move. The D.J. played *Under The Boardwalk* by the Drifters. The crowd of dancers slowed down. The heat from the hundreds of sweating, drunken lovers, and Ginny's warm breath washed over me. I put Anne's picture under a pillow, and gave myself over, as much as I could, to the night.

On the way back to the hotel, we stopped in at the arcade on the boardwalk and played air hockey. It was late. Only one of the five garage doors that opened onto the boardwalk was raised, and big black-steel fans in the corners stirred the cool ocean air. We were both pretty drunk, but we kept our heads down and had a good game. Ginny blasted the puck at me every time I gave her an opening, and before I knew it she had won. It was a lot of fun, and for the first time in a long time, I felt close to her.

She was, after all, a nice enough person. Crazy, but nice. And she liked me, which was half the battle. I though I had never really given her a chance. I sort of categorized her as not worth the trouble right from the start. Maybe, when she was comfortable, like she was walking on the boardwalk in the moonless night, holding my hand, she was someone I could love. Now that we were alone, away from Buchanan, away from what she thought other people thought, she was somehow different, more like a real person and less like a hungry puppy. I still probably could have snapped my fingers and made her jump, or said something harsh and made her cry. But I didn't want to. I don't know if she knew it, but I was as hungry as she was for some good normal fun, some pressureless companionship. There was room for compromise.

When we met freshman year, I had it all — the easy friendships, the confidence, the promising future. I had no reason to fall for a head case like Ginny. I deserved a perfect, whole person, someone who shared my way of looking at things, my enthusiasm. Things changed though, and now I didn't have nearly as much to give, nearly as much to loose. My checking account was empty, my grades were in the toilet, I was wrinkled and wandering, wondering, and smelled too much like cigarette smoke. It felt like compromise time. Maybe the two of use could prop each other up. Maybe something good could still happen."

We were back in front of the Oceanaire. Most of the lights in the rooms were out. The wind off the water was rustling the sea oats next to the boardwalk and the waves were rolling and breaking, thought you couldn't see them across the wide beach. It was time to make some kind of move. I thought for a second. I checked my belly. But there was nothing there, no desire. I was just tired.

I told Ginny I'd walk her back to her hotel. She kissed me and told me she loved me. I guess she thought I was being a gentleman. Hell, maybe I was. Maybe a gentleman is just a guy whose weariness or fear outweighs his desire. I held her hand and we walked off. I felt better, but I still didn't feel good.

After a while, we got to the stilt house Ginny and her gang had rented. They weren't in a sorority. They were affiliated, I guess, by their lack of affiliation. She kissed me again and told me to get some sleep. I said OK. She started up the steps and gave me a little wave before she stepped out of sight.

I started back toward the Oceanaire, but on the way back I remembered the dunes down the beach where Anne and I hid from everyone last year, where we figured out we loved each other. I couldn't remember the exact spot, so I walked out onto the sand and picked my way down the shore with nothing but some leftover streetlight to show the way. I found a place that seemed right. I plopped down in the sand and tried to remember how it was to have her next to me. I tried to picture her face in my head. It was weird. I couldn't do it. I could think of all the parts — her eyes, her nose and mouth — but I couldn't put it together.

CHAPTER FOURTEEN

I'd been feeling it for a while, but it was on the drive back from Myrtle Beach that I decided I was gonna leave Buchanan, even if I didn't fail out. It was the week after house party, and Ginny was back in my life as if the year and a half with Anne had never happened, as if she, Ginny, had been my girlfriend all along. She was quick that way. Before I knew what was what, she had some of her clothes hanging in my closet, eye shadow and lipstick in my dresser drawer, tennis shoes under my bed. The one big difference between now and when we first met freshman year was that she talked about Anne all the time. She told me she knew I had loved Anne, and that I had been hurt. She said she figured I probably still loved Anne, but that it was OK with her. She said you could love more than one person, and that as long as I loved her, she had no right to ask me to let go of Anne completely.

I thought to myself, "The bullshit is starting again." This was not the girl I walked with on the boardwalk in Myrtle Beach. There are certain rules, certain rhythms to relationships. And Ginny ignored them all. If she wasn't pushing me faster than I wanted to go into something I'm not sure I wanted, she was spouting nonsense like this Anne thing, telling me in effect that I could abuse her as much as I wanted and that she'd still be there for me. Didn't she know love takes time? Didn't she know love was an exclusive relationship?

If we were gonna stay together, things were gonna have to change. But that would take some time, and I didn't really have the energy. The term was almost over. Exams were coming, and if I was gonna leave Buchanan on my own terms, instead of at the Dean's invitation, I had some studying to do. The situation with Ginny would have to wait.

In the two weeks leading up to finals, I hardly saw Jay at all. He'd leave early in the morning and come back to our room late, after studying, after drinking with some of the new brothers. He seemed fine, even happy, but for some reason he avoided talking to me. Maybe he thought I was pissed at him for the way he handled the situation at Anne's house. I wasn't though. I know he tried to do what he thought was right. I know he was stuck between trying to be a good friend to me and honoring his long relationship with Anne. I understood that. I just wanted him to know I didn't blame him, and that I still considered him my best friend, even though we both knew I'd be leaving Buchanan in two weeks, and that we'd probably grow apart.

I don't know if it was because I knew I'd be leaving soon or because Ginny was always camped out in my room, reading her textbooks and movie magazines and smoking her menthols, but I spent a lot of my study time up on Paris Mountain, looking down on the campus. It was weird, but from a distance, I felt more like I was a part of the place. Something about seeing the whole set up — the clean brick and white buildings, the smooth green lawns, the uniform rows of hundred-year-old oaks — made that little world seem saner somehow, as if it all made sense, as if it were there for some reason other than to let kids in grown-up bodies come and make a mess of things.

Then I put my head down and read. Just read. I let it all go — everything that had left me so confused — and felt the spring sun on my legs and my face, and the cool breeze swirling from the other side of the mountain. I read in a way I'd never done before. There were no words or sentences, just a voice in my head, talking clear and loud, and making perfect sense. Three chapters of biology were chewed and digested by the time my stomach reminded me of the ham biscuits in my pack.

After lunch, I read for another hour and then drove back down the mountain. Out of some sort of premature nostalgia, I took the long way around campus just so I could enter through the front gate.

I though about the way I felt when I came in that way for the first time with my parents. It was a beautiful place then, but with the clean new leaves on the oaks and dogwoods, and the flowers blooming everywhere you looked, it was even better now. I rolled through the picture perfect scene wondering why I couldn't be a part of it. Why couldn't I turn off the searching, wondering part of my self and just accept my advantages gracefully? I mean, there was nothing forcing me to leave. It was my own choice. Dad would have kept paying my tuition, as long as I improved my grades. And I could do that. That was no big trick. It would just take a little bit of concentration. Then I could move through this country club world as a member in good standing — not just a guest. I thought there was no real advantage to learning more than I already knew, exploring more than I already had. What I needed was to forget some things, develop a little bit of trust. Trust in God. Trust in the American way. Take the pressure off myself.

Later that same afternoon, I climbed to the top floor of the library and studied in a lonely carrel until it was almost dark. Half asleep, I wandered out across the library lawn, down the brick steps where I gave Anne my Merrill Lynch money, through the rose garden that was in full bloom and smelling as sweet and perfumy as a department store beauty counter, and into the dining hall. The place was pretty quiet since it was almost eight o'clock.

I rounded the corner and saw Jay standing at the end of the line, waiting.

He didn't see me walk up. I grabbed a fork from the hopper and poked it into his ribs to get his attention. He turned around, smiling. When he saw it was me, his mouth kept smiling, but his eyes changed. I guessed I was right about him trying to avoid me.

"Hey, stranger," I said.

"Hey, Jimmy. What's up?"

"Nothing. Just been studying."

"That's good," he said awkwardly. "Guess we could both do with a little of that." His eyes were wandering around the big room.

"Listen, you know I'm not mad at you, don't you? There's nothing you could've done about Anne and . . . "

He was quiet.

"That's the problem between us, right?" I continued. "You thinking I'm pissed? Well, I'm not. I'm not. Look." I smiled an exaggerated smile, stepped forward, and held my palms out like a guy who just finished a tap dance.

He was still quiet, but he smiled a half-sad smile.

"Jesus," I said, "I hate to think I'm gonna loose you too. I mean, there's nothing I can do about Anne. I know that now. And even if I get straight As on my exams, the best I can do is get outta here with a C minus average. If we can't patch things up, these past two years will be a complete loss. Tell me what I can do. You're my best friend. You sorta owe me that much."

"Would you give it a rest? Man, I can't believe how much you think about yourself. If anybody spent half as much time thinking about you as you think they do, they wouldn't have time for anything else. You put so much pressure on yourself to be liked, to be a great friend, a great guy, that you're starting to drive people away. That's not the way friendship should go. It's got to be looser, easier. Nobody wants to make any long- term commitments. A guy just wants someone to drink beer and shoot the shit with. You're great at that, and that's how you oughta keep it. I'm your friend, Jimmy — but I can't make every decision in my life based on how it's gonna effect you. I don't wanna hurt you, or ignore you, but I've got my own shit to tend to."

I stood there kinda stunned. I felt like sitting on the floor and crying. I couldn't believe it. Was I pushing too hard? Maybe I was, but Jesus, it was only because I cared.

My brain went hot, and suddenly I felt completely isolated. All loyalty was gone, and Jay was just standing there peering at me, as if to say "come on, come on, say something, shit head." Somehow, at that moment, I thought about Ginny, how she'd react. She'd probably say something like, "I'm sorry. I was wrong to put pressure on you. I know you have other things to think about and that you can't factor me in to every decision you make. And it's OK. I'm here for you when you need me. Buddy. Sir. Savior."

I could taste the acid from my stomach boiling up in the back of my throat, and I rebelled. I was no pushover, no Ginny. And if Jay didn't think he had room for a friend like me, well then he could go to hell. I stood there and stared at him, and then it came out, it boiled out. "Fuck you," I said.

Jay was still peering at me — quietly. And then he nodded his head in a slow, deliberate way, and said, "Fuck you, too." He said it almost as if he were relieved to get it out, to have said it. Or maybe he was relieved I'd said it.

I stood there dumbly, waiting for my brain to do something. When it did, my body went right along, and I slapped the tray out of Jay's hands and across the room. His silver fell clinking, and his water glass chattered shrilly on the concrete floor.

Jay just stood there. I turned and walked.

CHAPTER FIFTEEN

In the last few days before exams, I quit communicating altogether. Everything good about Buchanan had slipped away from me. When I walked, I lowered my eyes and watched my dirty Adidas bounce in and out of my field of sight. Squirrels bounded through the leafy treetops and sprinted across the lawn, clearly not giving a damn about anyone but themselves.

Each morning, I stopped by the dining hall early and filled my backpack with peanut butter and jelly sandwiches and half pints of milk, and then walked slowly and alone to the library and climbed the stairs to the top of the stacks, to that same carrel, where I spent the whole day reading and memorizing and keeping my mind off myself. When I found myself thinking of how things could've been, I forced myself to think about my fight with Jay, or picture Anne with her hair cut short, standing in a dingy, loose fitting wedding dress at the alter next to a fat, 50 year old man in a three-piece suit (all lawyers were black-and-white Perry Masons to me). The pain would bring me back to the books. I forced myself to look at the bad. I was trying to learn how to forget.

My first exam was in biology. And it was the first time since I'd started at Buchanan that I was completely ready for any test. In that silent, crowded classroom, I turned the test paper face up and let my eyes dart over the pages. I knew immediately that I'd get every answer right. Information pushed and elbowed its way to the front of my brain. My only limit was how fast I could push a pencil. For a while I re-lived the feeling of complete confidence, a feeling that straightened my spine and narrowed my eyes. But as I walked out of the classroom thirty minutes later, my perfect paper smoking at the bottom of the professor's stack, I realized that this was a different brand of confidence, the kind that any slob with the minimal will power it takes to sit and study can have, the kind of competitive confidence that is measured against others, the confidence that comes from being better and quicker and smarter. It was different from my old stuff, the confidence that embraced everything new and wished everyone well, the kind that rested on self-security, the kind that grew without having to be watered every day. This new imposter, I realized, could be snatched any time you turned your back.

After I left the classroom building, I walked over to the fountain that separated the classroom buildings and the library. I sat on the marble edge and felt the warm sun on my face and the mist blowing off the airborne water. Whatever feeling of accomplishment I had faded when I remembered that even if I had aced the test — which I had, I knew — I'd be lucky to get a B minus when the grades from earlier in the term were averaged in. I just wanted to sit for a while, just sit until everyone else was done with their exams and a came walking out of the building. I though I'd like to go back to the library and study. But I had promised Ginny I'd meet her at the Stump for a beer, and I figured it would take more energy to blow her off and have to explain later than it would to just show up for a little while and then excuse myself.

So after a little while, I drove off campus and parked. I pushed my way through the heavy wooden door and into the dark loud room. *Roxanne* by the Police was cranking, and I heard a gang of girls laughing and yelling — obviously buzzed.

I stood there, waiting for my eyes to adjust. After some time, figures started to appear, and I searched for her blonde hair. I checked the booths first. Ginny could usually be found against a wall or in a corner, as if some private centrifugal force was always at work on her. But the only blonde, the only skinny one with hair down past her shoulders, was at the loud table in the center of the room. I figured I was a little early, or that she'd been hung up, so I walked over to the bar. But then the loud girls exploded into laughter again, and somewhere in that unsteady chorus, I heard Ginny's soprano giggle.

I ordered and paid for a mug of Bud, and then walked over toward the girls. As I got close, I was able to pick out faces, and I saw that these were the fraternity girls. Every one of them dated a brother. Some of them were in sororities, some weren't, but I knew that this was an even tighter, more exclusive group. I knew this primarily because I'd heard Ginny gripe about how snooty and standoffish they were, and how she'd like to see them all go to hell.

But Ginny had obviously changed her mind because when I walked up, it took a second to catch her attention, she was so busy laughing and hugging her new buddies. Some of the other girls motioned to her with their eyes or with head nods, and when she saw me she covered her mouth with her hand, and all the other girls were silent too, and looking at each other anxiously. Then they all burst out laughing again. They were having the damndest time.

When they finished laughing, Ginny said, "Hey, pumpkin." The rest of the pack said hello too.

"How'd your test go?" I asked, feeling kinda shaky speaking in front of an audience.

"OK," she said. "How 'bout you?"

I gave her the wink and nod equivalent of an A-OK.

"Good," she said. "If you keep it up, you won't have to transfer."

"I never said I had to transfer," I said, kinda pissed she raised the subject in front of the other girls. My academic struggles, though I knew they were kinda notorious, were none of their business. I thought about telling her that I intended to leave anyway — not because I was being forced out, but just because I was tired of this place, tired of her, tired of everything at Buchanan. I held my tongue though. I didn't want to nix her membership in the girls' club any sooner than I had to. Whatever I felt about Ginny, no matter how often she pissed me off, it was never my intention to ruin her fun.

"Do you have time to sit for a while?" she asked, pushing herself unsteadily up in her chair.

"Naa," I said, motioning for her to sit back down. "I thought I'd get right back on the horse — American Lit the day after tomorrow."

"OK," she said.

"You guys drink one for me."

I drank down the rest of mine and then turned to walk away. Then I thought of something.

"You seen Jay around?" I asked.

Ginny shook her head.

"Any of ya'll seen him today?" I asked the table.

They all shook their heads.

I spent the rest of the day in my cell in the stacks. Around 10:30 I packed it in and started back around the lake toward the house. It was a quiet, moonless night, and the stars were shining brighter than I thought they could. It was the kind of night where you could see so much of space — not just the stars themselves, but the patterns and waves they formed, the broad brush strokes — so much that you felt you were out among it, so much that you could sense the smallness and roundness of the Earth under your feet.

Back at the house, I walked through the front room, past a couple of guys and their dates drinking beer and watching the end of a Braves' game. I waved and then walked straight upstairs.

When I got to my room, I didn't knock. I took out my key and let myself in quietly, not wanting to disturb Jay if he was already asleep. When I went in though, I saw that the light was on and that Jay's bed was empty. My bed wasn't empty though. Ginny was in it. She was sleeping on top of the blankets, wearing jeans and my fraternity jersey, a closed geology text and an open Mademoiselle magazine beside her. Her forehead and closed eyes were smooth and completely relaxed, her lips tensed just enough to form a vague smile. She looked as if she had just completed the most satisfying day of her life, as if she had been awarded a prize or had won a race or had fallen in love or (and this was it) had become part of something she had been eyeing jealously from the outside.

This wasn't like Ginny. I mean, it was weird to see her satisfied, enjoying the present without obsessing on the fact that in a couple of days exams would be over and I'd be gone, and that with me would go her ticket to the inner circle. Was it that she was learning — learning to enjoy life more and worry less? Except for that short, late night in Myrtle Beach, I couldn't think of another time in the two years I'd known her when she was so relaxed. As I watched her sleep, the thing I couldn't figure was whether she was satisfied because something good had happened (could I be that important to her happiness?), or whether it was because she had learned to open herself up to the good things that had been circling around her all along.

I stripped down to my boxers and a T-shirt and walked down the hall to brush my teeth. When I got back, I shut off the lights and crawled into the bed with her. She woke halfway and snuggled up to me like a lonely cat. I liked her best when she was asleep.

I wasn't sleepy yet, so I just thought. Hell, my grades were on the way up, and I liked the fraternity. Jay was going through something I couldn't identify, but he was still my best friend, and we'd get it back together. And to hear Ginny talk, this was the first time she'd been happy since she'd hit puberty. Maybe that was enough. For the first time, I gave serious thought to staying. But somehow, without knowing exactly when or why or how, I'd already said good-bye.

CHAPTER SIXTEEN

My last exam came three days later — modern world history. And just like with my other finals, I was more than ready. I had a 40-page, hand-written outline of dates and places and people completely memorized, and everything else completely blocked out. I had my pencils sharpened and my blue books grouped in a crisp new manila folder. Ginny had already finished up, so she was probably out at the mall with some of the other girls, shopping for something good to wear to the end-of-the-year blow out.

Jay hadn't slept in the room for over a week (like he was avoiding me in particular), and when I allowed myself to think about it, my stomach got tight, and I wanted to cry. After everything that had happened, I couldn't believe he'd let one stupid argument screw things up for good.

I was walking across campus in my pre-exam trance, wearing shorts and a T-shirt, with a sweater tied around my waist in case the classroom was cold, when I saw Jay hopping out of Bob Jackson's beat up Celica, giving it the two bang on the roof thank-you before

Bob drove off. I called out Jay's name, but he kept walking as if he didn't hear me. I yelled again, louder, and this time he turned around and gave me the head nod that let me know he saw me. I hurried up beside him, and when I caught up, he started walking, and I walked along with him.

Before I could say anything, he said, "Listen, Jimmy. I'm in kind of a hurry here. Would you mind if we talked later?"

"Sure," I said. "I know you got a final. I just wanted to make sure you were OK. I mean, it's been over a week since . . . ."

"Jimmy," he cut me off as we pushed through the heavy door leading into the classroom building. 'I really can't get into this now. Can't we talk later?"

"OK," I said, getting kinda pissed at his attitude, like I was trying to bug him on purpose. "Will you be at lunch after this?"

"Yeah."

"I'll see you there then," I said.

"OK. Good luck on your test."

"It's under control," I said.

My test was two essays. I used up all three hours of the exam period. I could've quit after about an hour and a half and still pulled an A, but I knew a lot more than I needed, and somehow I felt the need to put it all down. This was my last chance, my parting shot, and I wanted my professor to know, I wanted somebody to know, that there was a brain, a person at the end of that long trail of Cs and Ds. They called me unmotivated, but now that I was surfing the front face of the bell curve, I figured it was they who were unmotivated. I had reasons for my non-participation. I was young. I had my mind on a million other things. But college, academia was their business, and they were the ones passing out As to people with only the barest, most superficial knowledge of the subject matter.

As I sat there in that quiet classroom, I wrote those essays with hate in my heart, hate for those bastard who presumed to grade me, to label me, hate for those happy, unquestioning dean's-listers who learned only what they were taught and wrote only what the professor wanted to read. I hated the characters in my essays — the Hitlers, the FDRs, the two-dimensional cartoons, the dragonflies with their wings pinned back, who represented just one thing each, not real people, not a cocktail of greatness and evil and boredom and unexplored talents. I hated myself for knowing more that I had been taught and not being able to leave it alone. I hated needing someone to know, someone to notice. Like a dog pissing on a fence post, I hated having to prove myself, prove I was here, listening and thinking.

When I walked out of the classroom building, away from the test, I felt a strange kind of peace. Good or bad, it was all over, and all I had to do was pack up my things and throw them in my car and that would be it.

It was a clear and sunny and warm outside, and somehow, though I was a whole day's drive from home, I could smell the ocean on the breeze. I wanted to be home right then, not to see my family or my old high school buddies, but just to park my car on the side of the road and walk barefooted through the palm fronds, dodging the sand spurs, over the dunes and down onto the beach.

But I wanted to catch up with Jay at the dining hall too. I wanted to get him into the car and drive to the pool hall down town. Drink some beers. Get away from the pressure. Make things right.

As I walked, I looked at all the smiling faces. Exams were over and the campus swarmed with happy mugs. I thought about how easily people forgave. I mean, judging by all the happy faces, you'd've thought every one of them had straight As. But you know that's not true. So what makes the C and D students smile? Just knowing it's over for a while? That's probably true for a lot of them — but at some point you realize you're getting pushed into a corner. Even if it's your own fault, even if you never study, even if you're begging for it, you can't fail until the professor says you fail. And that's what's hard to forgive.

It's the professors who lower the booms, it the professors who close their minds and give their heads little shakes as they drop your paper into a lettered bin, even though if they took the time to think, the time to care, they'd know that letter wasn't you. But expecting someone to care is expecting too much. And that's what I figured those smiling faces knew. Expect nothing and you won't be disappointed. Well I expect something, and when I don't get it, I don't forgive. They had no choice? I had no choice. None of us have any choice.

When I got to the dining hall, Jay was nowhere around. Hardly anyone was around. The steam trays were full of macaroni and cheese, fried okra and breaded veal patties, but there was no one to eat it. The kitchen crew sat around with their heads in their hands, speaking quietly, looking at me as if I were the last to hear the news, whatever the news was that was keeping everyone away. I walked back outside, and the campus was suddenly empty except for a few stragglers scrambling for their dorms like kitchen roaches when the light flips on.

I walked slowly around the lake, looking back on the campus for what I figured would be the last time. Everything was still and brightly lit, like in a postcard. The breeze confused the reflection of the campus in the lake. As I rounded the last bend and took the trail into the trees, I started to hear David Allen Coe's strong hick voice pushing through the branches, and I realized the party at the house had already started. I guess I just wasn't thinking.

I emerged from the woods and crossed over the street. I moved up the front walk and up the porch steps. Even though I knew the names of everyone in sight — the guys playing Frisbee on the lawn, the girls giggling on the porch rail, the fellows on the roof in bathing suits with zinc oxide on their noses — I felt like an outsider, like an old man walking through the neighborhood where he spent his childhood.

I thought about Marty Lansdowne, the way he'd walk into the house like he owned the place. He was still a student, but his visits were rare, and when he showed, he walked like royalty, greeting everyone but not really talking with anyone. I thought I had become like him in a way. But now that I was looking at things from sorta the same angle as Marty, I thought that maybe that calm friendly manner may not have been confidence at all. It may have been embarrassment. Maybe he felt the jabs, the prickly sting that comes from straying off the well-stomped path, the sting I was feeling for not staying at Buchanan, for not sticking with it, for quitting. Maybe Marty was no better that anyone else, maybe his life was a big joke just like everyone else's. Maybe the confidence I thought I saw, the inner peace, was an act. Maybe . . . .

No. No. I hated to think of Marty as anything but perfect — no, not perfect, but enlightened. If he felt confidence, then confidence was correct. If he felt embarrassment, then that, no doubt, was right.

I walked straight through the house and out back to the parking lot to see if Jay's truck was around. It wasn't. I bounded up stairs to see if I could pick up some clues, see what was going on. And as I let myself into our room, somehow I could tell — from the smell, the feeling, the shunt of the dead bolt clicking free as I turned the key — that he was gone for good. I looked around the room and discovered I was right. His cloths, his books, everything was gone.

On the shelf by the bar there was a bottle of Cuervo tequila with a little bit left in it. I grabbed it, hopped up on the bar and took a swig. What the hell was he running from? Did his need to avoid me outweigh his desire to stick around and enjoy the after-exam party, to see all folks he wouldn't see all summer?"

And why lie? Why tell me you're gonna meet me for lunch if you know damn well you'll be halfway to Georgia before noon?

I took another swig. I looked around the room. I noticed my bed had a small pile of things Jay had borrowed in our two years together — an old harmonica, some socks, an L.A. Dodgers cap. There was something else too. I hopped down off the bar and took a look. It was a T-shirt with a noted pinned to it. I unfolded the shirt and realized it was Jay's Easthampton football shirt, the one he couldn't bring himself to give to charity. Then there was the note.

"Jimmy," it started. "Sorry I had to leave without saying goodbye. I got some personal things I need to take care of. I'm also sorry about some of the things I said and the way I've been keeping to myself these past couple weeks. Believe me when I say it has nothing to do with you. I thought it did once, but now I know it doesn't. Anyway, I've really enjoyed hanging out with you these past two years. You're as good a friend as I've ever had. Good luck. You deserve it. Your buddy. Jay."

I sat on the bed and thought about the note. After what we'd been through together, what possible problem could he have that he couldn't tell me about? Maybe he just knew I wouldn't be around to help him see it through, so he decided to keep me out of it from the start? That wasn't Jay though. He wasn't that calculating. That's one of the main things I liked about him. Whatever his problem was, that note made me feel a lot better about things. I took another swig.

Half an hour later I realized I was still sitting on the edge of the bed. The bottle of Cuervo was gone. Then a strange thing happened. For the first time that term, the first time since Anne had left, I put all the bad luck I had been nursing on a shelf and resolved to have a good time. I figured moping around one day more or less wasn't gonna make any difference. I decided to celebrate, partly out of nostalgia for the way things used to be (something I could still conjure up if I closed my eyes and thought back), partly because the opportunity presented itself, but mostly because of what Jay said in that note. Maybe it wasn't me. Maybe I wasn't making all this crap happen.

Things happen all the time that aren't my fault. It rains, it snows. Presidents are elected. People die. None of it is my fault. Maybe the same thing is true of Anne. Maybe that whole mess was just a run of bad damn luck. That was my hypothesis of the day, and right or wrong I was gonna stick with it. I peeled off my shirt, replaced it with Jay's football jersey, and headed out into the sun.

CHAPTER SEVENTEEN

By the time the sun dipped behind the tree tops, I was sore from an afternoon of Frisbee and touch football. I was also fighting off a mid-party beer headache. Everybody was helping out, getting ready for the real party that would start around eight. I pitched in and helped carry the couches and coffee tables and other front-room furniture into the kitchen to make as much room as possible for dancing. When everything was set and the first two kegs were tapped, when the rest of the guys went upstairs or back to their apartments to get cleaned up and dressed, I went out on the porch and rocked.

It was around dusk, and the evening was clear and warm. The traffic up and down the street was a steady parade of cars full of whooping students and loud stereos, trucks overloaded with pledges and kegs, and, on the sidewalk, girls in shorts and sports shirts, with their hair curled and their faces made up, walking.

I still hadn't heard from Ginny.

Finally, from out of the traffic an old Volvo slowed down and pulled over. And from out of the back seat, Ginny appeared. She didn't see me at first. She stood for a second on the sidewalk in front of the house and looked up at my window. She didn't look like she was dressed for the party. Her hair was pulled back into a ponytail, and she was wearing jeans and one of my T-shirts. I whistled to get her attention. She looked over and waived, but she wasn't smiling. As she walked across the lawn, I could tell she had something on her mind. When she got close, I asked how she was and she said something I couldn't quite make out. The last word sounded like "wreck."

"Did you say you were in a wreck? You OK?" I said, even though it was plain to see she wasn't hurt.

"No," she said. "I said 'I'm a wreck.' I'm OK. Nothing happened to me. It's just that I heard something, something you should know — at least something I think you should know."

She leaned on the rail in front of me and looked into my eyes as if she were trying to see the back of my skull.

A jolt of guilt ran through — as if Ginny were my mom, as if I were about to be confronted with some sin. "What is it?" I said. "What's going on?"

"I know this isn't my business," she said, "but did you get Anne pregnant?"

I didn't say anything.

"You have to believe me," she said. "It's important. I hope you say no, but if the answer is yes, you have to tell me."

I couldn't imagine what the problem was. Was Ginny gonna dump me because of something I'd done when we weren't even dating? And since when did I even care what Ginny thought about me? I couldn't figure out what kind of trouble I was looking at."

"Tell me!" she shouted.

I stalled a couple of seconds longer, but then I gave up. "Yeah," I said. "It was a mistake, but Yeah."

This time she was silent.

I thought about asking why she wanted to know, but something told me I wasn't gonna like it. Something else told me I'd find out anyway.

"You know Liz Donovan, Bill Porter's girlfriend?"

"Sure," I said, nodding.

"You know she works at the clinic?"

"No," I said. "But I believe you."

"Well I ran into her this afternoon, and she said she handled a phone call from a doctor in Atlanta. An obstetrician. He needed some records on a patient of his."

I looked at Ginny. I wasn't breathing.

"It was Anne," she said. "The patient was Anne. She checked into the Fulton County Hospital this afternoon. The maternity ward. It looks like you're going to be a father."

Before the news completely hit me, I was upstairs packing. Ginny had begged me to take her along, and since I'd already promised her a ride back to Florida, I told her OK. I told her I expected her to be packed and on the stoop in an hour, no excuses, and she ran back to her dorm.

It was going to be weird having her with me, but I figured I owed her something. She didn't have to tell me about Anne. She could've sat on the information. She didn't have anything to gain by telling me. In fact, she had everything to loose. Somehow, without actually going through the logical steps, I figured that if I couldn't bring myself to feel deeply about Ginny herself, at least I could share something with her that I felt deeply about. Anne was certainly one of those things.

By the time I had everything packed and ready to go, the party had already started. I pulled my car up to the back steps, popped the trunk, and in five or six trips I had everything packed. I ran up stairs to have one more look around the room. There was some dirt and dust and a few empty beer cans on the floor. There was the beat up couch Jay and I had paid fifteen bucks for at the Salvation Army. If things had been different, I would have cleaned up, I would have taken care of the details. As it was though, I tossed my room keys on the floor and left the door open. I bounded down the stairs and out the back door. I jumped in the car, turned over the engine and was gone. No goodbyes. Something from Tom Petty's red album was cranking.

As I drove over to pick up Ginny, I felt a strange calm. The panic I felt when I first found out Anne was pregnant didn't return. All the options, the variables, the what ifs had been eliminated, and all that was left was to face the truth. In a way, I felt like an outsider. I had to keep reminding myself that this was happening to me. I thought back to the day I peddled out to Marty's cabin. Back then, all I wanted was a way out. I didn't get my wish. Whether Anne wanted it or not, I was back in it deeper that ever.

Just before I turned the last corner leading to Ginny's dorm, I considered wheeling around and heading for Florida — alone. Ginny was the only one who knew I knew about Anne, and I doubted she'd spread it around that I ran out. With any luck, Ginny'd just decide I was an asshole and forget all about me. Hell, I thought, it wasn't even running out. Anne obviously had no intention of letting me know what was going on. I could just act like I never knew, and nobody would ever be able to prove different. Anne took my Merrill Lynch money, she told me she would go to the clinic and have things taken care of. After she dropped out, I called her and wrote her, and I even chased her down to Atlanta. She's the one who cut me out. No one could accuse me of running.

I had a chance to make a clean break. But I couldn't. Not for any high moral reason. I just couldn't. I was caught up. The choice — if there was one — was made without me. Lots of choices had been made without me. And I wanted, I needed, to know the result.

I rounded the final corner, to the rear of the girl's dorm, and my headlights fell on Ginny standing next to her things. There was enough to fill the back of a pick-up — suitcases and a stereo, a small refrigerator and hefty bags full of cloths.

Instead of kicking up a fuss, I just pulled over, hopped out and silently crammed everything into the back seat. Ginny didn't say a word as she got in the car, but her eyes were darting back and forth, and I knew there was no end to the angles she was figuring.

CHAPTER EIGHTEEN

I was on Interstate 85 again, rolling through the night. All I could hear was the hum of the tires. All I could see was the road and the sky and the truckers' tossed cigarettes that burst into limp fireworks on the asphalt.

Ginny sat next to me, wide-awake and thinking. She was always thinking.

"You ok?" she said.

"Hmm?"

"You alright?"

"Yes."

"What are you thinking about?"

"Not much of any thing."

"What can I do to help? I want to help."

"Nothing. I don't know why you insisted on coming along."

"Shoot me. I'm interested," she said. "I love you."

"I don't have the energy to play with you. And I certainly don't need any more love. That's what got me into this mess in the first place."

"Do you still love her?"
"No."
"Do you think she still loves you?"
"No. I don't know."
"Will you love the baby?"
"I don't know. Please shut up."
"You can, you know. You can love the baby without loving her. It's your baby too, and you have just as much right to . . . ."
"Shut up. I'm begging you."

Two and a half hours after leaving Buchanan, we pulled into a parking space at the hospital. I hopped out and started walking toward the main entrance. Behind me I heard Ginny's door click open and then, a couple of seconds later, slam behind her. I heard her footsteps, and then felt her hand take hold of mine.

The hospital was enormous — tall and angular, with glass panels and exposed steel girders. It could have housed a bank, a corporation, the phone company, CNN. But this was a hospital, and that became apparent when the front door retracted automatically and I was confronted with a burst of artificial atmosphere — cooler and heavier than the real air outside, and carrying with it the smell of disinfectant and iodine, cigarette smoke and rubbing alcohol, dust and cooking grease, and somewhere in that cocktail, a dash of death.

Without my having to ask, Ginny split off and took a seat in the waiting area. At the desk I spoke Anne's name. The old man wearing a pink blazer adjusted his bifocals, kicked his head back, and consulted his clipboard, moving his shaky hands down the page.

"Room 918. Elevator's over there," he finally said.

When the elevator door opened on the ninth floor, I heard a chorus of crying babies. I followed that call down the hall to the plate glass window behind which the next generation of southern gentry incubated. A tired-looking nurse behind the window looked at me as if to ask if she could help direct me to my child. I looked back dumbly. Where one of these mine? I didn't know. I wasn't sure I wanted to know.

I stood for a while and thought nothing, but then finally the number 918 elbowed its way back to the front of my brain, and I shuffled off down the hall. When I got to the room, the door was closed. I stared at it, but I couldn't knock. I pictured her in there alone and in the dark, in pain, swearing revenge against me, the way I'd deserted her.

Then, suddenly, there was a nurse behind me.

"You here to see Miss Anne, darling?" she asked as she opened the door.

"I . . . Aaah."

"Come on in. She'll be glad to see you."

I walked into a bright room and saw her on the bed. Her hair seemed longer now, was brushed back and tied up in a red bow. Her face was wrapped up in a big cordial smile, and across her legs, below her bulging stomach, there was a stuffed bear the size of a golden retriever.

"Jimmy. Hi. Come in. Come in," she said. "Mom. Dad. Say hi to James Macy, Jay's fraternity brother."

Across the room, by the window, stood her mom and dad, champagne glasses in their hands, all smiles and nods. I don't know if I was smiling, I couldn't feel my face.

"Sir. Ma'am.

Without speaking, Anne's father turned his back to me. I glanced at Anne and she still had that same smile going, but for an instant she shot me a faint, pleading look with her eyes. Then her father wheeled around again. He had an extra glass of wine in his hand. He walked toward me and said: "Join the party, son," and handed me the drink.

"Yes, sir. Thank you."

"Dispense with the sir crap, son," Anne's dad said. "The name's Bud. And this here's my bride, Leigh."

"Hello, James," She said.

Just then, I felt an arm around my shoulder. It was Jay. "Hey buddy," he said. "What brings you to this neighborhood? He smiled and dug a playful knuckle into my ribs. "Come over here and say howdy," he said. "You know my folks, John and Eydie."

"Sure," I said. "Good to see you again."

Jay leaned heavily on my shoulder, letting me do the balancing for both of us. John and Eydie didn't smile. They didn't speak. They just looked at each other. Then Dr. Newton's face kinda twisted and Mrs. Newton and him busted out laughing. Dr. Newton slapped his knee and the forward motion nearly carried him out of his chair. They were both pickled as hell. In fact, everybody in the room except the nurse and Anne were flying high.

Jay had his face right up next to mine. The smell of Jack Daniels was unmistakable. "Ain't they the scariest looking bunch you've seen in your life? God help this new one. He's gonna have to learn to pour a drink before he learns to finger paint."

I set Jay back up on his own feet, and I went over to Anne's bed and took her hand. "How you doing, Sweetheart?" I said.

"Fine. Just fine," she said, with that same broad grin still on her face.

I couldn't think of what to say. I shifted my eyes down to her bulging stomach. She wore a flannel nightgown, and her belly had hundreds of teddy bears holding balloons all over it.

"It won't be long," Anne said. "The contractions have already started."

"And you're sure you're ok? I mean, the baby's . . . ."

"Oh, hell yes," she said. "My little quarterback's gonna run for extra yards any time now."

She looked genuinely peaceful. I wondered what the doctor had her on. Where was the pain? Where was the fear? Where was her memory of me, of my whole part in this celebration?

We all just sat quietly for a while. Everybody sorta watched me watch Anne. Then the nurse, who had walked out, came back in again. The old folks traded looks and then burst out laughing again. The nurse, who didn't seem to mind the hilarity, but then again had her job to do, shooed me off the bed and hovered over her patient.

Then, as I stepped away from Anne, I saw it. I don't know how I had missed it before. It was right there in front of me, right there on her puffy little finger. A ring. Two in fact. A big old diamond ring and a gold band. A gold wedding band.

I spun around and looked at Jay's hand. And there it was, clinking up against his glass of Jack Daniels. A shiny new wedding band. I'd walked into the middle of a damn wedding reception.

"Excuse me, folks," I said. "I think I need a cigarette. Jay, come keep me company." I spun him around by his shoulders and steered him out the door and down the hall and up against the wall.

"What'd you do?" I said in a whispery but angry voice.

"What'd I what?"

"The ring, man. The ring. You married her? My girl. My baby. You stepped right into my shoes, didn't you, you. . . ."

Jay was looking down at the melting ice in his glass.

"You could have told me. You could have warned me . . ."

"There was no reason to tell you anything," he said, in the same kind of whisper. "But now that you know, we're gonna need you to kinda play along."

I couldn't think of a thing to say. I just remember thinking that it was already done, and there wasn't anything I could do to change it. But that wasn't really true.

"Jimmy," he said. "This is how she wanted it. There was no use in her trying to rope you into doing something you didn't want.

It'd just end up causing trouble for both of ya'll, and it'd be the kid that'd end up paying."

He put his hand on my shoulder and turned me so he wouldn't have his back to the wall. "Jimmy, this is nothing against you. You did everything you could've. Anne told me you were never anything but a gentleman. But hell, I knew that already. You're a good guy, and I'm proud to be your friend. And if you think I'm doing you a favor, well, I'm glad to do it. And if you think I wronged you, then I'm sorry, because that was never our plan."

"What was . . . I mean, what is your plan?"

"To let you go. To let you do what ever it is that'll make you happy."

"What about you?" I said. "What business do you have getting married at twenty years old? You don't have the money to raise a kid."

"You don't need to worry about that," he said, relaxing a bit. "This ain't the first unplanned baby to drop in on the Newton Family. I guess I never mentioned it, but I came along about six months after my folks were hitched. Dad had just started at Emory dental, and they didn't have a pot to piss in. My grandparents helped out some, and everything shook out fine. Hell, its like my dad said today — he said there's no perfect time to have a kid, so you might as well just do it whenever. And the way I figure it, this whenever is as good as any other."

I didn't have anything else to say, so I just stood there. I could feel the energy coming off him, the excitement. He seemed so pleased, my natural impulse was to congratulate him. But I didn't. I couldn't. All I could do was stand there. And for some reason Jay seemed a little bigger, a little older, and a lot more like a grown-up man. The sense I got was of a man who had taken his position and was determined to stick to it regardless of whatever was going to happen, a kind a sweet, simple-minded courage. It seemed like a dumb way to handle your life, but I couldn't help being a little envious. He'd taken my mess and made it into something to get excited over.

CHAPTER NINETEEN

Thinking back, I don't really remember Anne saying or doing or being anything that special. It was like she was just a beautiful carnival mirror, and I was taken by the reflection of myself I saw in her. From the start, it was a lot more about me than it was about her, or even us. Maybe that's why I never thought she'd do something like this. Maybe I never really knew her. Maybe I never really loved her.

So I was twenty and leaving the Carolinas, leaving Buchanan, heading back to Florida with a girl I barely knew, a girl I barely cared about. I swear, if she had gotten out of the car at the next rest stop and walked off into the woods, I can honestly say I could have got into the car and kept heading south and never have given her another thought. I just didn't care. I couldn't care. Not about Ginny, not about Jay and Anne, not about the baby, and not that damn much about myself. I wanted to be by myself. I didn't want to look for anything new to care about.

I thought about how things had been with me just two years ago, when I was driving the other way on Interstate 95 with my parents. There was a lot I wanted to know, a lot I wanted to do. Well I knew it. I'd done it.

You know, when you're young, you see things, you hear things — ways of looking, acting, thinking — and you choose among them, taking what looks good, and then those things become you. Then, when you're older, you sometimes want to shed those things. But you can't. It's as if you are forced to wheel around a cart containing everything you picked up as a boy — odd nuts and bolts, torn baseball cards, rubber bands, those little metal knockouts you find on construction sites that look like faceless coins. It's all you. So it's natural, I guess, when it all seems too much, too heavy, you react by quitting. You stop acquiring. Everything new is just more trouble, more to worry over, more to be held accountable for. And what you already have, you sort into piles and store away, and you stand guard over them, and that's it.

Made in the USA
San Bernardino, CA
26 October 2016